WHEN THE RADIO WHISPERS

FROM WAVES TO THE BEYOND

Charles Etheridge

First Edition 2025

Publisher: MK Storyworks
Cover and Interior Design: MK Storyworks
Author: Charles Etheridge

ISBN: 978-1-80700-000-4

TABLE OF CONTENTS

DEDICATION

To the pioneers of the invisible spectrum—the early radio engineers who first listened to the airwaves, and the seekers who were brave enough to believe they heard more than static.

And in memory of **Barnaby Crowthorne,** the brilliant mind whose vision was corrupted, and whose redemption now guides the Luminous Society.

AUTHOR'S NOTE

When the *Radio Whispers: From Waves to the Beyond* was born from a fascination with the intersection of science and the supernatural that defined the early 1920s—a time when radio technology was revolutionizing communication even as spiritualism reached unprecedented heights.

The core idea is that electromagnetic waves might carry more than just human voices—they might carry consciousness itself. The character of **Vespera Luminaire** was inspired by the real women who pioneered radio engineering during this period. Her synesthetic perception of electromagnetic fields symbolizes the kind of extraordinary sensitivity that could perceive a world beyond sound.

I dedicate this story to the power of human consciousness and the courage it takes to fight for free will, even against forces that claim absolute, rational control. The boundaries between the occult and the scientific are thin; the Luminous Society exists to ensure they are never breached again.

Charles Etheridge

HISTORICAL NOTE

When **The Radio Whispers** is set in October 1923, during a pivotal moment in both broadcasting history and the spiritualist movement. The story unfolds against the backdrop of the early BBC, which had begun daily radio transmissions from London's 2LO station in November 1922 less than a year before our tale begins.

In 1923, radio technology was still in its experimental stage. The BBC operated from Marconi House on the Strand, using primitive vacuum-tube equipment that required considerable technical expertise to run effectively. Night-shift engineers like Vespera often worked alone, fine-tuning receivers and transmitters in darkened laboratories filled with glowing tubes and crackling electrical apparatus. The electromagnetic spectrum was far less crowded than it is today, making it easier to detect unusual signals or to imagine that mysterious transmissions might come from supernatural sources.

This period also marked the height of the post-war spiritualist revival. The devastating losses of World War I and the 1918 influenza pandemic had left millions searching for evidence of life after death. By 1923, an estimated 14 million people across North America and Europe were "occasional or frequent" spiritualists, served by thousands of churches, mediums, and séances. Even prominent figures like Sir Arthur Conan Doyle had become passionate advocates for spirit communication.

The convergence of these two phenomena emerging electromagnetic technology and widespread belief in spiritual communication created a singular cultural moment. Many spiritualists truly believed that radio waves and the "etheric vibrations" used by mediums operated on similar principles. The invisible, seemingly miraculous nature of radio transmission made it easy to imagine that the same airwaves carrying news and music might also carry messages from the dead.

The scientific concepts explored in this novel though dramatized for narrative purposes are grounded in genuine 1920s electromagnetic theory. The "collector's" equipment, while fictional, draws inspiration from real experiments conducted with radio-frequency apparatus and early inquiries into the electromagnetic nature of human consciousness. Even Thomas Edison announced plans in 1920 to build a "spirit communication device," though he never completed it.

While When The Radio Whispers is a work of supernatural fiction, it reflects real questions that fascinated both scientists and spiritualists of the time: What is consciousness? Can it survive physical death? And might the invisible forces that carry our voices across great distances also carry something far more profound?

Charles Etheridge

PROLOGUE

October 15th, 1919
BBC Experimental Laboratory, London

The electromagnetic coils hummed with barely contained energy as Dr. Barnaby Crowthorne made his final adjustments to the apparatus. Across the laboratory, his research partner, Dr. Cornelius Blackthorne, watched with growing agitation, his pale hands gripping a leather notebook filled with calculations that bordered on obsession.

"Barnaby, you must reconsider," Cornelius said, his cultured voice tight with barely suppressed excitement. "The spiritual realm isn't meant for mere communication it's a source of unlimited power waiting to be harvested."

Crowthorne paused in his work, electromagnetic patterns dancing before his eyes like living aurora. After months of research, he had finally achieved stable contact with consciousnesses existing beyond death voices that spoke through radio frequencies, proving that human awareness could survive bodily dissolution. It was the greatest scientific breakthrough in human history.

And his partner wanted to weaponize it.

"The spirits trust us, Cornelius. They've shared their knowledge freely and helped us understand the electromagnetic nature of consciousness itself. I won't betray that trust by trapping them for experiments."

"Trust?" Cornelius laughed, a sound without warmth. "They're energy patterns, Barnaby. Fuel for discoveries that could make us gods among men. Think of what we could achieve with unlimited spiritual energy at our disposal!"

The apparatus sparked, and both men felt the familiar tingle that indicated spiritual contact. Through the modified radio equipment, a gentle voice emerged Eleanor Crowthorne, Barnaby's wife, dead these past three years from consumption.

"My darling," she said, her words formed from frequencies that shouldn't have carried human speech. "Something is wrong. I can sense Cornelius's intentions through the electromagnetic field. He's been building something terrible."

Barnaby's blood chilled. "What kind of something?"

"A machine designed to trap us to feed on our spiritual essence. The other souls are frightened. He's already tested it on some of the weaker spirits. They've been... consumed."

Cornelius stepped forward, his face transformed by predatory hunger. "Eleanor, my dear sister-in-law. How convenient that you've chosen to manifest tonight. You'll be the first full-scale test subject for my collection apparatus."

He moved to a second control panel one Barnaby hadn't

noticed before, hidden beneath a laboratory cloth. The device beneath was a grotesque hybrid of scientific precision and occult symbology: brass coils wound in patterns that hurt to look at directly, vacuum tubes glowing with sickly green light, and electromagnetic generators that distorted the air itself.

"Cornelius, no!" Barnaby lunged toward the device, but his partner was ready.

The collection apparatus roared to life, its electromagnetic field crackling with malevolent purpose. Eleanor's voice rose to a scream that echoed through both audible and spiritual frequencies a sound of pure agony as her consciousness was torn from the ethereal realm and imprisoned within Cornelius's machine.

"You monster!" Barnaby grappled with his former friend, but Cornelius had prepared for this moment. A knife appeared in his hand, its blade inscribed with symbols that seemed to drink the light from the laboratory's electric bulbs.

"I'm sorry, old friend, but you lack the vision to appreciate what we've accomplished. Don't worry your wife's spiritual energy will power discoveries that will revolutionize human understanding of death itself."

The blade struck true, and Barnaby collapsed beside his equipment, his lifeblood pooling around the electromagnetic coils. With his final breath, he reached for the apparatus's emergency shutdown and triggered a feedback loop that sent uncontrolled energy surging through the laboratory.

Sparks flew. Chemicals ignited. Within minutes, the room was ablaze. Cornelius gathered his notes and the portable collection device, leaving Barnaby to burn along with all evidence of their research.

As he escaped into the London night, Dr. Cornelius

Blackthorne smiled with satisfaction. The official investigation would conclude that both researchers had perished in an accidental laboratory fire. But Cornelius would continue their work alone, perfecting the techniques to harvest spiritual energy from both the living and the dead.

Behind him, the BBC laboratory burned like a pyre, consuming the last traces of Barnaby Crowthorne's benevolent research. In its place, something far more sinister had been born a collector of souls who would spend the next four years preparing for a harvest that would shake the foundations of life and death themselves.

The flames cast dancing shadows on the October sky, and those sensitive to such things might have noticed that the shadows moved with purpose as if the fire itself had become a living entity, hungry for human consciousness.

The age of the collector had begun.

1

SPECTRAL TRANSMISSION

The electromagnetic waves danced before **Vespera Luminaire's** eyes like ribbons of golden light, each frequency a distinct hue in the spectrum only she could perceive. It was nearly midnight on **October 15th, 1923** exactly four years since **Barnaby Crowthorne's** mysterious disappearance from this very laboratory. Alone in the BBC's experimental radio division, Vespera worked under the soft hum of electricity, her synesthetic gift transforming the invisible world of radio waves into a symphony of color and motion no other engineer could see.

The anniversary was no coincidence. Vespera had specifically requested this shift, hoping the date might somehow guide her toward a breakthrough in replicating Crowthorne's lost work. His research into electromagnetic phenomena had been decades ahead of its time, but when he vanished, all his notes and equipment had disappeared with him.

The receiving apparatus hummed with current, its vacuum tubes glowing amber in the dim laboratory. Vespera adjusted the frequency dial with practiced precision, watching as the colors shifted from deep violet through blue and into the cool greens she associated with long-wave transmissions. Most wireless operators relied solely on sound, but her synesthesia gave her an almost supernatural ability to fine-tune reception.

For the past hour, she'd been trying to reach the experimental station in Edinburgh, but atmospheric interference kept breaking the connection. The patterns she could see told her something unusual was happening in the electromagnetic spectrum that night waves that shouldn't exist threaded through normal radio traffic like silver veins through marble.

As the clock on the wall neared midnight, Vespera made one final adjustment. The receiving coils sparked with blue fire, and suddenly the air itself seemed to crystallize around her. The electromagnetic patterns shifted into something that made her breath catch not the chaotic scatter of ordinary interference, but **organized structures pulsing with deliberate rhythm.**

"Hello?" she whispered into the microphone, though she wasn't trying to reach any earthly station. "Is someone there?"

The response came not through the speakers but through

her synesthetic perception **colors forming words, frequencies spelling out impossible messages:**

We can see you, Vespera Luminaire.

Her hands trembled as she steadied the controls, desperate to maintain the connection. In four years of radio work, she had never encountered anything like this. The electromagnetic patterns were too precise, too purposeful to be natural.

We have been trying to reach you. The one who hunts grows stronger, and you are in danger.

"Who are you?" she asked, her voice barely audible in the empty room. Outside, London slept, unaware that within this small laboratory, the boundary between science and the supernatural was dissolving.

The colors shifted again, forming new, unmistakable patterns:

Lady Evangeline Ashworth. I died three days ago, but I am not at rest. None of us are.

Vespera's rational mind reeled. **Lady Ashworth's death had been front-page news** a tragic fall from her hotel balcony. But this was impossible. The dead couldn't transmit radio signals. Yet the evidence pulsed before her eyes in frequencies no living being could produce.

You must listen carefully. There is a collector who hunts women with gifts like yours. He uses electromagnetic equipment to trap souls, and he has marked you as his next acquisition.

The laboratory's lights flickered. For a moment, Vespera felt an unseen presence watching her from the shadows. Fear crawled up her spine, but she forced herself to stay focused.

"What kind of gifts?" she whispered.

You can see what others cannot. Your synesthetic perception makes you valuable to him, but it is also what might save you. Do not trust men with silver canes. Do not work alone after dark. And find Aurelius Grimwald he can help you understand what you are truly facing.

The connection began to fade, the colors breaking apart like dispersing smoke. Vespera frantically turned the dials, trying to hold onto the signal.

Remember the collector strikes when his victims are isolated and vulnerable. We will try to reach you again, but the electromagnetic pathways are dangerous. He monitors them, and our time is

The transmission cut off abruptly, leaving only the familiar static of empty airwaves. The lights steadied. The sense of being watched slowly ebbed away. But Vespera remained frozen at her desk, staring at the radio apparatus with a mixture of awe and terror.

She glanced at the clock **12:07 a.m., October 16th.** Seven minutes that had changed everything she thought she knew about the world.

With trembling hands, she began writing everything she could remember frequencies, wave patterns, every word of that impossible conversation. Her scientific discipline demanded documentation, even if her mind struggled to comprehend it.

Yet one thought refused to leave her: **Lady Ashworth had known her name.** She had been reaching out to Vespera specifically. Which meant that somewhere in London, a collector of souls had already marked her for death.

The empty laboratory suddenly felt perilously exposed. For

the first time in four years of night shifts, Vespera found herself eager to leave the BBC building. She gathered her notes, powered down the equipment, and headed for the door.

Behind her, the radio apparatus gave one last spark of blue light a farewell... or perhaps a warning that the conversation was far from over.

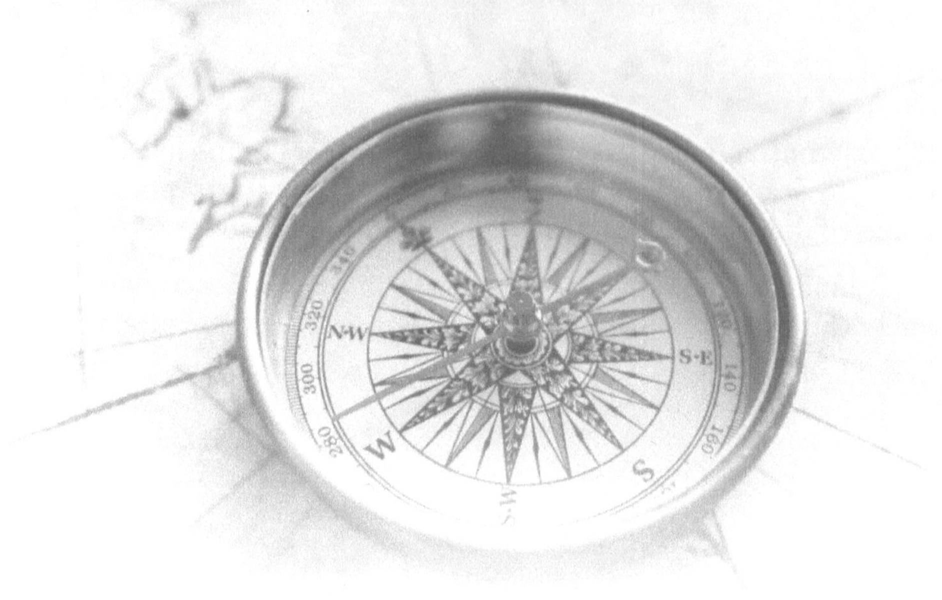

2

THE VOICES IN THE ETHER

Vespera barely slept that night, her mind racing with possible explanations for what she had experienced. By the time she returned to work the following evening, exhaustion battled with scientific curiosity. She had spent the day at the British Library researching electromagnetic theory, spiritualism, and every account she could find about Lady Ashworth's death, but conventional sources offered no explanation for impossible radio transmissions from the dead.

The laboratory felt different somehow charged with a potential energy that made her synesthetic perception more acute than usual. Colors appeared brighter, electromagnetic patterns more intricate. She set up her equipment with nervous anticipation, wondering if the previous night had been an elaborate hallucination brought on by overwork and anniversary anxiety.

At precisely 11:43 p.m., the apparatus came alive with familiar silver patterns threading through the normal radio traffic. This time, she was ready.

"Lady Ashworth? Are you there?"

The response formed in crystalline clarity across her synesthetic vision:

I am here. But I am not alone tonight.

New patterns joined Evangeline's signal different colors, different rhythmic structures.

Margaret Whitmore. I died two weeks ago. They said it was a suicide, but that is a lie.

Catherine Frost. A month ago. He made it look like an accident.

Three voices. Three impossible transmissions from three dead women. Vespera's hands moved automatically, adjusting frequencies to maintain the connection while her rational mind struggled to process what was happening.

"How is this possible?" she whispered.

The collector has equipment that can trap and manipulate spiritual energy, Evangeline explained. Electromagnetic resonance at frequencies your science hasn't yet discovered. We exist now as energy patterns conscious but imprisoned.

He's coming for you next, Margaret's signal interjected. Tomorrow night. He's been watching you, learning your routines. You work late, alone. You're perfect prey.

The laboratory lights began to flicker, and Vespera felt that watching presence again stronger this time, more malevolent. The silver patterns in her vision started to waver and distort.

He's found our transmission, Catherine warned.

A new voice cut through the spiritual communication, cultured and amused:

"My dear Miss Luminaire. How delightful to finally make your acquaintance."

The electromagnetic patterns shifted dramatically, and Vespera saw something that defied all reason a face formed within the radio frequencies, aristocratic features composed of light and shadow.

"Allow me to introduce myself. I am what your spirit friends call the collector, though my true name is far more distinguished. I've been quite looking forward to meeting you."

Vespera's finger hovered over the power switch, but something held her back scientific fascination warring with primal terror.

"You're him," she breathed. "The one who killed them."

"Killed is such a crude word. I prefer to think of it as transformation. Your three friends are now part of something far grander than their mundane existences could have provided. They power my great work a machine that will revolutionize the understanding of consciousness itself."

The face in the frequencies smiled with predatory charm. "And you, my dear, will be the crown jewel of my collection. Your synesthetic abilities will allow you to perceive the full beauty of what I'm creating."

Don't listen to him! Evangeline's voice cut through the collector's transmission. He's a monster who feeds on spiritual energy! Run!

"Such dramatics," the collector said dismissively. "Miss Luminaire, I'm offering you the chance to be part of scientific history. Think of what we could discover together the nature of consciousness, the electromagnetic properties of the soul, the intersection between spirituality and science that your Barnaby Crowthorne only began to explore."

At the mention of Crowthorne's name, Vespera's blood ran cold. "You knew him?"

"Knew him? My dear girl, I collected him first. His research was fascinating, but his execution was flawed. With your help, I can perfect what he began."

The laboratory filled with an oppressive presence, and Vespera felt invisible eyes studying her with the intensity of a spider examining a trapped fly. The electromagnetic patterns around her began to shift into configurations that hurt to perceive directly.

He's trying to mark you! Margaret warned. Break the connection now!

Vespera's hand slammed down on the power switch, cutting all transmission abruptly. The laboratory plunged into ordinary darkness, lit only by the gaslight from the street outside. Yet she could still feel him a malevolent attention fixed on her location.

She gathered her notes with trembling hands, her mind made up. The morning's research would have to wait she needed answers, and she knew exactly where to start. Aurelius Grimwald, whoever he was, had been mentioned by name in Lady Ashworth's first message. If he could help her understand what she was facing, she had to find him.

As she prepared to leave, the wireless apparatus gave one final crackle of static. Through the speakers, barely audible, came the collector's voice:

"Until tomorrow evening, Miss Luminaire. I do so hate to keep a lady waiting."

The building suddenly felt like a trap, and Vespera fled into the London night unaware that, from the shadows across the street, a figure in an expensive overcoat watched her departure with satisfaction. The game was beginning, and he did so enjoy the hunt.

3

THE ANTIQUARIAN'S SHOP

The next morning found Vespera standing before a narrow shop in Bloomsbury, its dusty window displaying an eclectic collection of curiosities that seemed to span several centuries. The painted sign above the door read *"Grimwald's Curiosities Rare Books & Antiquities,"* but something about the place suggested it dealt in far more unusual merchandise than books alone.

After hours of searching through London directories and questioning locals, she had finally located the shop. Her scientific skepticism warred with desperate hope she needed answers, and conventional sources had failed her completely.

A small brass bell chimed as she entered, and Vespera found herself in a dimly lit space that seemed larger than the building's exterior dimensions should have allowed. Shelves stretched up to surprising heights, filled with books, instruments, artifacts, and objects she couldn't readily identify. The air smelled of old leather, brass polish, and something else a subtle electromagnetic charge that her synesthetic senses picked up as faint golden threads weaving through the atmosphere.

"Miss Luminaire, I presume?"

She turned to find a tall, pale man emerging from the shadows between the shelves. He appeared to be in his forties, with prematurely silver hair and remarkable green eyes that seemed to see far more than they should. His clothing was well-tailored but slightly old-fashioned, as if he had stepped out of an earlier decade.

"How do you know who I am?" she asked, instinctively stepping back.

"Several ways, actually. Your electromagnetic signature, for one people who work extensively with radio equipment develop a distinctive resonance that lingers in their aura. Your synesthetic perception, for another you're currently seeing the protective wards I've woven throughout this shop as golden threads, aren't you?"

Vespera's eyes widened. The golden patterns she had noticed were indeed following specific pathways around the shop, forming a complex geometric design.

"Those are… intentional?"

"Quite intentional. They keep out unwanted spiritual

influences and help me identify individuals with true psychic sensitivity." Grimwald gestured for her to follow him deeper into the shop. "I've been expecting you since yesterday evening. The collector's interest in you has created quite a disturbance in the ethereal frequencies."

They passed shelves lined with instruments that looked like hybrids of scientific equipment and mystical artifacts brass compasses that pointed toward magnetic orientations defying physics, telescopes with lenses that seemed to reveal more than visible light, and devices that hummed with the same electromagnetic charge Vespera could perceive as color.

"Lady Ashworth told me to find you," she said. "She said you could help me understand what I'm facing."

"Lady Evangeline was a remarkable woman intelligent, perceptive, and, unfortunately, exactly the type of individual the collector finds irresistible." Grimwald stopped before a locked cabinet and began selecting various items. "She came to me three weeks ago, convinced someone was stalking her. I gave her protective amulets, but they proved insufficient against the collector's advanced methods."

He handed her a silver medallion inscribed with symbols that seemed to shift and change when she wasn't looking directly at them. "Wear this at all times. It won't stop him, but it will make it harder for him to track you through electromagnetic resonance."

Vespera fastened the medallion around her neck, surprised to feel an immediate sense of... protection? The sensation was hard to describe like standing under a sturdy umbrella in threatening weather.

"What exactly is the collector?" she asked. "The spirits said he traps souls using electromagnetic equipment."

"The collector is what happens when scientific brilliance becomes corrupted by obsession," Grimwald replied gravely. "His real name is Dr. Cornelius Blackthorne I knew him years ago, before his transformation. He was Barnaby Crowthorne's research partner, but while Barnaby sought to communicate with spiritual realms, Cornelius became obsessed with controlling them."

The name hit Vespera like a physical blow. "Dr. Blackthorne? But he died in the laboratory fire that killed Crowthorne!"

"So, the records claim. In reality, Cornelius caused that fire to cover his theft of Barnaby's research. He's spent the past four years perfecting techniques to trap and manipulate human consciousness after death." Grimwald's expression grew darker. "He's building something he calls the Eternal Engine a device that will allow him to achieve immortality by consuming the spiritual energy of others."

"And he needs people with psychic abilities to make it work?"

"Precisely. Your synesthetic perception of electromagnetic fields makes you particularly valuable. You can see spiritual energy directly, which means you could potentially control his equipment if properly trained."

Grimwald moved to another cabinet, withdrawing what looked like a modified compass. Its needle spun wildly, pointing in directions that changed every few seconds.

"Electromagnetic disturbance detector," he explained. "It will warn you when the collector or his equipment is nearby. But Miss Luminaire, you must understand you cannot face him alone. He's accumulated considerable power over the past four years, and his victims' trapped souls only make him stronger."

"Then what am I supposed to do? Hide for the rest of my life?"

"Build an alliance. There are others who understand what we're facing mediums, investigators, even some progressive scientists who've begun to accept that consciousness might not be purely biological." He handed her a card with an address written in elegant script. "Mrs. Minerva Blackheart conducts séances in Camden. She has genuine psychic abilities and has been trying to communicate with the collector's victims."

Vespera studied the card, her mind racing through possibilities. "Could she help me contact the spirits directly? Without using the radio equipment, he might be monitoring?"

"Possibly. But be warned direct spiritual communication is dangerous. The collector can trace those connections, and Mrs. Blackheart will be putting herself at considerable risk."

As if summoned by their conversation, the electromagnetic disturbance detector in Vespera's hands began spinning frantically. Grimwald immediately moved to the shop's windows, closing heavy curtains that blocked not just light but seemed to muffle sound and other sensations as well.

"He's nearby," Grimwald whispered. "Stay absolutely still."

Through the shop's walls, Vespera could hear footsteps on the cobblestone street measured, confident, approaching. The electromagnetic patterns her synesthesia revealed began to shift and darken, as if something malevolent was casting shadows across the invisible spectrum.

A cultured voice drifted through the walls, carrying an impossible distance.

"Good afternoon, Miss Luminaire. I know you're there.

Such a fascinating conversation you've been having with our mutual friend."

The voice paused directly outside Grimwald's shop.

"I do hope you're not planning anything foolish. The game is so much more enjoyable when my quarry provides appropriate sport. Until tonight, my dear."

The footsteps continued down the street, fading into the normal sounds of London traffic. Yet the electromagnetic disturbance detector continued spinning for several minutes before finally settling.

"He knows about this place," Vespera said quietly.

"He knows about everything that might help you. Which means we have very little time to prepare." Grimwald gathered additional items from his cabinets vials of salt mixed with metallic powders, crystals that seemed to generate their own electromagnetic fields, and a small device that looked like a radio receiver tuned to spiritual presences rather than radio waves.

"Take these. Learn to use them. And Miss Luminaire" he met her eyes with an expression of grave concern "whatever you do, don't try to face him tonight. He's expecting that, planning for it. Survive until tomorrow, and we can begin teaching you to fight back."

As Vespera left the shop, her arms full of protective artifacts and detection devices, she couldn't shake the feeling that she was walking into a trap. The collector had let her find Grimwald, had allowed their conversation to continue. Which meant either he was supremely confident in his abilities, or he wanted her to believe she had allies and hope.

Neither possibility was particularly comforting as she

stepped back into the London afternoon, now armed with knowledge that made her situation seem even more desperate than before.

4

DEAD AIR

Detective Inspector Marcus Nightingale stood in the morgue of London General Hospital, studying the body of Lady Evangeline Ashworth with growing unease. According to the official report, she had fallen from her hotel balcony during a charity gala a tragic accident witnessed by dozens of society guests. But after three similar deaths in the past two months, he was beginning to suspect something far more sinister.

"No signs of struggle, no indication of foul play," said Dr. William Holbrook, the chief medical examiner, as he pulled back the sheet covering the victim. "But there's something unusual I wanted you to see."

Nightingale leaned closer. Lady Ashworth had been a beautiful woman of thirty-five, known for her wit and charitable work. In death, her features were peaceful, almost serene which was unusual for someone who had fallen four stories onto stone pavement.

"Look at her hands," Holbrook instructed, lifting the victim's right arm.

The inspector frowned. The fingertips showed unusual burns not from impact or fire, but circular marks that looked almost like electrical burns. Similar marks appeared at her temples and behind her ears.

"Electromagnetic scarring," Holbrook said quietly. "I've seen similar patterns on workers who've been electrocuted by industrial equipment. But Lady Ashworth wasn't near any electrical apparatus when she died."

"What about the other victims Margaret Whitmore and Catherine Frost?"

"Identical markings. All three women died from their falls, but all three had been exposed to some form of electrical energy shortly before death." The doctor's expression grew troubled. "Inspector, in my professional opinion, these women were incapacitated before they fell. Someone used electrical equipment to render them unconscious, then staged their deaths as accidents."

Nightingale made notes, his mind turning over the implications. Three women, all from London society, all with similar electromagnetic injuries. But what kind of equipment could cause such precise damage? And why hadn't any witnesses reported seeing electrical devices at the death scenes?

"Dr. Holbrook, I need you to compile detailed reports on all three victims. Focus on those electromagnetic injuries exact patterns, probable voltages, anything that might help us identify the equipment used."

As Holbrook nodded and began preparing his materials, Nightingale pulled out the newspaper clipping about Lady Ashworth's death that he'd been carrying for days. Something about the witness accounts had been nagging at him several people had mentioned that she seemed to be "listening to something" before she fell, as if hearing sounds no one else could perceive.

Electromagnetic equipment that could incapacitate victims from a distance. Strange auditory experiences before death. Precise targeting of society women with no apparent connection except their social status.

In the margin of his notes, he wrote: **"Radio engineer electromagnetic connection?"**

The BBC had several wireless operators who worked with high-powered transmission equipment. If someone was using radio-frequency devices as weapons, they would need considerable technical expertise to pull it off and access to equipment sophisticated enough to affect human physiology.

"Dr. Holbrook," he called as the medical examiner prepared to leave, "one more question. Could radio equipment cause injuries like this?"

"Standard broadcasting apparatus? Unlikely. But theoretical applications of electromagnetic radiation could certainly affect human nervous systems. There was a researcher named Barnaby Crowthorne who was exploring such possibilities before his death four years ago."

"Crowthorne? I remember that case a laboratory fire, wasn't it?"

"Indeed. But his research notes were never recovered. There were rumors he'd developed techniques for using electromagnetic fields to influence human consciousness."

Nightingale felt the pieces clicking into place. "Where can I find information about Crowthorne's work?"

"The BBC would have records he was consulting with them on experimental radio applications. And there's an antiquarian in Bloomsbury, Grimwald, who deals in scientific artifacts. He might know something about Crowthorne's equipment."

As the inspector left the hospital, his mind was already forming a plan. Three dead women, all with electromagnetic injuries. A missing researcher whose work had involved consciousness manipulation. And somewhere in London, someone with access to advanced radio equipment was hunting society women with surgical precision.

He would start by interviewing the BBC's radio engineers particularly anyone who worked with experimental equipment during nighttime hours. If his theory was correct, the killer was someone with intimate knowledge of electromagnetic manipulation someone who could strike from a distance and leave no conventional evidence.

The October afternoon was growing dark as Nightingale hailed a cab toward Broadcasting House. He had no way of knowing that less than a mile away, a young woman named Vespera Luminaire was receiving warnings from the very victims he had been studying or that the killer he sought was preparing for his next strike.

But as his cab wound through London's streets, the detective felt the peculiar sensation that he was racing against time toward a confrontation with forces that challenged everything he thought he understood about murder, science, and the nature of death itself.

At Scotland Yard, the evening shift was just beginning. In a few hours, when Nightingale returned with his initial findings, he would discover that the case he thought he was investigating was only the surface of something far stranger and far more dangerous than conventional crime.

The dead, it seemed, were trying to warn the living. The question was whether anyone would listen in time.

5

THE FIRST TRANSMISSION

Minerva Blackheart's séance parlor occupied the ground floor of a narrow Victorian house in Camden. Its windows were draped with heavy burgundy velvet, and the interior was lit by candles that cast dancing shadows on walls lined with occult paraphernalia.

To most of London's respectable society, Minerva was either a charlatan preying on the grief-stricken or a dangerous practitioner of dark arts. The truth, as usual, was more complicated.

At forty-five, Minerva had been conducting séances for nearly two decades ever since a stage accident had ended her promising career as a music hall performer. What began as an act of desperation using her theatrical skills to comfort the bereaved while earning enough to survive had gradually evolved into something far more genuine and infinitely more dangerous.

She possessed what Aurelius Grimwald called *"the true sight"* an ability to perceive spiritual presences that went far beyond clever showmanship or cold reading techniques. It was a gift she had initially resisted, then reluctantly accepted, and now wielded with the precision of a seasoned professional.

That particular evening found her seated at her circular table with Mr. Harold Pemberton, a railway clerk seeking contact with his recently deceased wife. The séance was proceeding normally Minerva had indeed made contact with Mrs. Pemberton's spirit when the atmosphere in the room suddenly changed.

The temperature dropped by several degrees, causing the candle flames to flicker wildly. The spirit communication board between Minerva and her client began moving of its own accord, spelling out words that had nothing to do with Mrs. Pemberton.

D-A-N-G-E-R... H-E... C-O-M-E-S...

"Mrs. Blackheart?" Mr. Pemberton's voice wavered as the planchette moved frantically beneath their fingertips. "This isn't my Margaret speaking, is it?"

Minerva's trained instincts screamed warnings. The presence forcing its way into her séance wasn't Mrs. Pemberton's gentle spirit this was something desperate, powerful, and immediate.

"Mr. Pemberton, please remove your hands from the board," she instructed firmly.

The moment their contact ceased, the planchette flew across the board with violent speed:

THE LUMINAIRE WOMAN... HE SEEKS HER... TONIGHT...

All the candles guttered out simultaneously, plunging the room into darkness. But Minerva's psychic senses could perceive what her client could not three distinct spiritual presences had materialized in the parlor, their energy crackling with desperate urgency.

"Mrs. Blackheart?" A cultured female voice spoke from the darkness. "I am Lady Evangeline Ashworth. I pray you can hear me clearly."

Even in death, the aristocrat's reputation preceded her. Mr. Pemberton made a strangled sound of recognition.

"I hear you," Minerva replied steadily. "What do you need?"

"There's a woman Vespera Luminaire, a radio engineer. She's in mortal danger tonight. The collector has been watching her, studying her routines. He plans to strike when she's alone and vulnerable."

"The collector?"

"The monster who murdered me, who murdered Margaret Whitmore and Catherine Frost. He traps our souls, using our spiritual energy to power some hellish machine he's building."

A second voice joined in older, more authoritative. "Margaret Whitmore here. The collector uses electromagnetic equipment to disorient and control his victims. He strikes when they're isolated, then stages their deaths as accidents."

"Catherine Frost," came a third, younger voice. "I can sense Miss Luminaire through electromagnetic residue she's at the BBC building right now. But he's there too, watching from the shadows."

The spiritual energy in the room was building to dangerous levels. Minerva could feel the strain on the three trapped souls as they forced themselves to maintain contact across the barriers between life and death.

"How can I help?" she asked.

"Find Aurelius Grimwald," Evangeline's spirit instructed. "He understands what we're facing. The collector's true name is Dr. Cornelius"

The connection shattered abruptly as a new presence slammed into the séance circle like a physical blow. The temperature plummeted further, and frost began forming on the windows despite the mild October weather.

A cultured male voice spoke through the speakers of a wireless set that shouldn't have been receiving any transmissions.

"My dear Mrs. Blackheart. How very impertinent of you to eavesdrop on my collection."

Mr. Pemberton tried to rise from his chair, but an invisible force held him motionless, his eyes glazing over with supernatural compulsion.

"You're him," Minerva breathed, fighting against the psychic pressure bearing down on her consciousness. "The collector."

"Indeed. And you, Mrs. Blackheart, possess exactly the sort

of psychic sensitivity I've been seeking. Such a waste to see true mediumistic ability squandered on parlor consolations."

The wireless crackled with static, but the voice remained mockingly clear. "I have a proposition. Surrender willingly, and I'll make your death swift. Your abilities would make an excellent addition to my apparatus."

"Never."

"How predictable. Very well then, we'll do this the difficult way."

The psychic assault intensified, and Minerva felt her consciousness being pulled from her body. But she had learned protective techniques over the years. With tremendous effort, she focused on the silver ward carved into the table's underside a precaution she had taken after encountering malevolent spirits in Whitechapel.

The ward blazed with protective energy, and the collector's grip loosened momentarily.

"Clever," his voice admitted. "But such protections are temporary. I know where to find you now, Mrs. Blackheart. And when I've finished with the Luminaire woman, I'll return for you."

The hostile presence withdrew abruptly, taking the unnatural cold with it. The gas lamps flickered back to life, and Mr. Pemberton slumped in his chair, blinking in confusion.

"What happened? Where's Margaret?"

"Your wife is safe, Mr. Pemberton, but others are not." Minerva was already moving toward the coat closet, her mind racing through necessary preparations. "I'm afraid our session must end. There's someone I need to find before it's too late."

"But I barely spoke with her"

"The dead can wait, Mr. Pemberton. It's the living who need our help now." She pulled on her coat with quick, efficient movements. "Go home. Lock your doors. And if you encounter a gentleman with a silver-topped cane, avoid him completely."

Before the bewildered clerk could respond, Minerva was already striding purposefully through the Camden night. She had two urgent tasks: reach Grimwald's shop for protective supplies, then find Vespera Luminaire before the collector claimed another victim.

The October sky was clear and cold, stars visible despite London's gaslight haze. But Minerva's psychic senses detected something else in the atmosphere, an electromagnetic tension that made the very air feel charged with malevolent purpose.

As she hurried through the maze of London streets, she couldn't shake the feeling that she was already too late. The collector had been methodical and successful in his previous hunts. What could possibly be different about tonight?

Then she remembered Evangeline's urgent message: Miss Luminaire possessed abilities that might save her. Perhaps, for the first time, the collector had chosen prey capable of fighting back.

The thought gave Minerva hope as she disappeared into the London night, racing against supernatural forces to prevent another soul from joining the collector's gruesome tally.

Twenty minutes later, she burst through the door of **Grimwald's Curiosities,** the antique bell announcing her urgent arrival. She found the proprietor in his back office, examining what appeared to be an ornate electromagnetic detector by lamplight.

"Aurelius," she called breathlessly. "We have a crisis. The trapped spirits they managed to contact me directly."

Grimwald looked up, his pale green eyes sharpening with characteristic intensity. "Let me guess they're trying to warn someone."

"Vespera Luminaire. She works at the BBC, and the collector is moving against her tonight." Minerva paused to catch her breath. "The spirits said you'd know what to do."

"Miss Luminaire was here yesterday. Remarkable woman synesthetic perception of electromagnetic fields. She already made psychometric contact with Lady Ashworth's belongings through her radio work."

"Then you understand what we're facing?"

"A man who has weaponized death itself." Grimwald moved to his locked cabinets, withdrawing protective artifacts silver medallions, vials of treated salts, and devices that detected spiritual presences. "The question is whether we can reach her before the collector completes his collection."

Minerva accepted the protective items, fastening a medallion around her neck. "He knows about me now used my séance circle to trace the spirits' communication."

"He knows about all of us. Which means we have precious little time to prepare." Grimwald locked his shop and turned the sign to *Closed.* "We need to reach the BBC building immediately."

As they stepped into the night, the electromagnetic detector in Grimwald's hand began spinning wildly, its needle shifting directions every few seconds.

"Massive spiritual disturbance," he muttered, studying the device's erratic behavior. "The collector is drawing power from his trapped victims, preparing for something significant."

He met Minerva's eyes with grim understanding. "I believe, Mrs. Blackheart, that we're about to discover whether the living and the dead can cooperate to defeat a monster who belongs to neither world."

The London night swallowed them as they hurried toward their desperate race against forces that blurred the boundaries between science, spiritualism, and survival itself.

They arrived at Marconi House minutes later, finding the front doors locked. The night guard checked his ledger and informed them that Miss Luminaire had signed out and left the building over an hour ago. However, Minerva's psychic senses detected a sharp surge of residual electromagnetic energy: Vespera hadn't left the area. She had somehow returned to the BBC building alone.

Grimwald swore under his breath, realizing the collector's trap had worked perfectly by dividing them. Vespera was now inside, facing the full force of Dr. Blackthorne's malice without their aid.

6

THE THIRTEENTH STRIKE

Vespera hadn't intended to return to the BBC building that night. After the revelations at Minerva's parlor learning that the collector was Dr. Cornelius Blackthorne, her predecessor's research partner who had supposedly died in the same laboratory fire she'd planned to follow Grimwald's advice and find somewhere safe to hide until they could formulate a proper plan.

But as she lay in her small Bloomsbury flat, staring at the ceiling while October 17th became October 18th, one thought kept returning: Barnaby Crowthorne's original research notes might still exist somewhere in the BBC's archives. If Blackthorne had been his partner, there might be clues about his methods, his weaknesses, even the original purpose behind the electromagnetic consciousness experiments. More importantly, if Blackthorne was monitoring radio frequencies, he would expect her to stay away from the BBC building. Going there might be the last thing he'd anticipate.

At 2:17 a.m., Vespera made her decision. She gathered her protective medallion, the electromagnetic disturbance detector Grimwald had given her, and the small vial of consecrated salt that Minerva had insisted she carry. If she was going to face a monster who used her own field of expertise as a weapon, she needed every possible advantage.

The night porter at Broadcasting House knew her by sight Miss Luminaire often worked unusual hours, and her security clearance gave her access to most areas of the building. He barely looked up from his crossword puzzle as she signed in.

"Working late again, Miss Luminaire?"

"Couldn't sleep," she replied truthfully. "Thought I'd catch up on some research."

The building felt different in the small hours of the morning. It was tomb-quiet now, with only the distant hum of electrical systems and the occasional creak of settling architecture. Vespera made her way to the archives in the basement, a maze of filing cabinets and storage rooms that contained years of BBC documentation. If Barnaby Crowthorne's research had been preserved anywhere, it would be here.

The electromagnetic disturbance detector in her pocket remained mercifully still as she searched through files labeled *Experimental Broadcasting* and *Research & Development* –

1919–1923. Her synesthetic perception revealed the normal electromagnetic patterns of the building regular, predictable, and reassuringly mundane.

She found Crowthorne's file wedged between reports on antenna design and transmission range experiments. The folder was surprisingly thin for someone who had supposedly been working on revolutionary consciousness research, but it contained enough to make her hands tremble as she read.

Most of the papers were technical specifications for equipment she didn't recognize. But it was a personal letter, tucked between two equipment diagrams, that made her blood run cold:

My Dear Cornelius,

I'm growing increasingly concerned about the direction our research has taken. The subjects we've tested the volunteers from Bedlam they're not the same afterward. Mrs. Hartwell hasn't spoken since the procedure, and young Timothy seems to be hearing voices no one else can perceive.

I know you believe we're on the verge of a breakthrough in consciousness manipulation, but I fear we're tampering with forces beyond our understanding. The electromagnetic field configurations you've developed don't just affect brain activity. They appear to be attracting... other things. Spiritual presences that may not have our subjects' best interests in mind.

I've decided to suspend the experiments until we can better understand the risks. I hope you'll support this decision, though I suspect you won't.

Your concerned friend,

Barnaby

The letter was dated October 10th, 1919 five days before

the laboratory fire that had supposedly killed both men.

Vespera's electromagnetic disturbance detector suddenly began spinning frantically in her pocket. The normal patterns her synesthesia showed her shifted, darkening, as if something malevolent were casting shadows across the invisible spectrum.

She wasn't alone in the archives anymore.

"Miss Luminaire." The voice came from directly behind her cultured and amused. "How refreshingly predictable. I was wondering when intellectual curiosity would overcome your survival instincts."

She spun around to find a tall, elegantly dressed man standing in the doorway. In his left hand, he carried a walking stick topped with an ornate silver head exactly as the spirits had described.

Dr. Cornelius Blackthorne. The collector. Very much alive.

"Death is such a limiting concept, don't you think? I prefer to consider myself... evolved." He stepped into the archive room, and Vespera saw the air around him shimmering with electromagnetic energy visible only to her synesthetic perception. "I see you've found Barnaby's correspondence. Such a cautious man, my dear partner."

"You killed him."

"I liberated him. Just as I liberated Lady Ashworth, Miss Whitmore, and Miss Frost. Just as I'm going to liberate you." Blackthorne's smile was warm and utterly devoid of humanity. "The Eternal Engine, my dear a device that will allow human consciousness to transcend the boundaries of individual existence."

He raised his walking stick, and Vespera saw electromagnetic energy gathering around its silver head like visible lightning. "Your synesthetic abilities make you particularly valuable. You can perceive the Engine's operation directly, which means you could help me refine its efficiency."

Submit, a voice whispered in her mind.

The consecrated salt Minerva had given her was in her left coat pocket. With her right hand, she grabbed the nearest metal filing cabinet, grounding herself while scattering the salt in a rough circle around her feet.

The effect was immediate. Blackthorne's electromagnetic attack broke against the salt barrier like radio waves hitting a metal screen.

"Clever," Blackthorne said, though his voice had lost some of its amusement. "But parlor tricks won't save you for long."

Instead of fleeing, Vespera did something that surprised them both. She pulled the electromagnetic disturbance detector from her pocket Grimwald's modified compass and hurled it at the archive room's electrical junction box. The device struck the switches with a shower of sparks, and every light in the basement went out at once.

She sprinted for the archive door, scattering more consecrated salt as she ran. Behind her, Blackthorne's cultured laughter echoed through the basement corridors.

"Excellent! I do so enjoy a challenge!"

Vespera reached the stairs and began to climb. Blackthorne wasn't limited by physical form anymore; he could travel through any conductive medium in the building.

She burst into her laboratory and immediately began setting up the radio apparatus. But as she reached for the transmission controls, every piece of equipment in the room suddenly came alive with that familiar blue fire.

Blackthorne's voice emerged from the speakers. "Did you really think you could outrun electromagnetic energy, my dear? This entire building is now my domain."

Vespera pressed the transmission key and spoke into the microphone. "This is Vespera Luminaire, broadcasting an emergency signal. Lady Ashworth, if you can hear me I need your help. All of you. I need your help now."

The radio equipment exploded with silver light. Three voices spoke simultaneously:

We are here. We have been waiting. Fight him, Vespera. We'll help you fight him.

The trapped spirits turned their own energy against their captor.

You made one crucial error, Cornelius. You kept us conscious. And conscious minds can learn to resist.

The collector's presence faltered, his confident control wavering for the first time. Vespera scattered the last of her consecrated salt across the laboratory floor and ran for the door.

Behind her, Blackthorne's voice rose into an inhuman shriek of rage. "You cannot escape me, Vespera Luminaire! I am electromagnetic energy itself now! I exist in every wire, every transmission, every spark of electrical current in this city!"

But as she reached the building's main entrance, Vespera heard the spirits' combined voices:

Find the others. Find Grimwald. Find the medium. The collector can be defeated, but only if the living and the dead work together.

The night porter was unconscious at his desk, overcome by

electromagnetic discharge. Vespera grabbed the building's master key from his belt and locked the main doors behind her as she fled into the London night.

She was halfway across the pavement when a figure stepped out of the fog directly into her path.

It was Detective Inspector Marcus Nightingale. He stopped short, his hand instinctively going to the small, occult-looking compass Grimwald had directed him to purchase, which was now spinning frantically in his coat pocket. He recognized Vespera from a distance the experimental radio engineer he'd planned to interview.

"Miss Luminaire?" he demanded, his voice sharp with professional urgency. "What in God's name is happening here? The building's lights are out, and the air feels charged."

Vespera rushed to him, grabbing his arm. "Inspector, you were looking for answers about the electromagnetic scarring? I have them. The killer is Dr. Cornelius Blackthorne Crowthorne's partner. He's alive, he's using the building's wiring as a weapon, and he's building something called the Eternal Engine." She thrust Crowthorne's letter into his hand.

Nightingale stared at her disheveled state, the silver medallion at her throat, and the raw fear in her intelligent eyes. Then he looked back at the darkening, crackling BBC building. He remembered the morgue reports, the precise burn marks, and Holbrook's speculation about consciousness manipulation.

"A silver-topped cane," he murmured, recalling the witness descriptions of the collector. "And his name is Blackthorne." He dropped his hand from his pocket, the rational investigator giving way to the man who had just seen the impossible confirmed. "Where is he headed?"

"He's been watching me. He knows I have allies. We need

to regroup with Grimwald and Minerva Blackheart. We need to find his engine now."

"Then we find his engine first," Nightingale said firmly, already moving toward the cab stand. "You lead the way, Miss Luminaire."

Vespera fled into the London night, but this time, she was not alone. The full alliance was now formed united by an impossible truth confirmed by science, spirit, and Scotland Yard.

7

THE SILVER TRACE

The four allies gathered in the dimly lit, artifact-filled back room of **Grimwald's Curiosities**. The meeting had been arranged with utmost secrecy, using a complex series of coded telegrams and route diversions that would have exhausted a lesser group. The objective was simple but terrifying: to use the meager evidence they possessed to locate the hidden laboratory of a monster who could manipulate consciousness itself.

Vespera felt the weight of her stolen letter and the lingering electromagnetic shadows from the BBC. Grimwald meticulously polished his protective medallions while consulting celestial charts that only he could interpret. Minerva sat at the periphery, her senses extended, listening for the faint, desperate whispers of trapped souls. Nightingale, the newest member, remained closest to the door, his posture that of a detective accustomed to danger, if not its current spectral form.

"We have four pieces of evidence," Nightingale summarized, tapping a pencil against a clean sheet of paper. "The forensic markings from the victims, the spirits' testimony, Miss Luminaire's encounter, and this letter from Crowthorne." He focused on Vespera. "The burn patterns the electromagnetic scarring were precise, almost surgical. Dr. Holbrook, the medical examiner, suspects that electrical equipment incapacitated them from a distance. The question is: what kind of equipment leaves a trace that faint?"

"Equipment designed to interact with the human nervous system at the subtle frequency of consciousness," Grimwald said, not looking up from his work. "Blackthorne isn't using brute voltage; he's using resonance. He's searching for a specific spiritual fingerprint."

Vespera stepped forward, laying a map of central London beside the evidence. "His primary method of communication is long-wave radio frequencies, but the presence I sensed at the BBC and the paralysis he tried to inflict suggests he's developed a powerful, directional transmitter. He's operating from a central, shielded location."

Minerva opened her eyes, wet with unshed tears. "The voices are fading, but I found something in the ether tonight a pattern of suffering that pulses with immense electrical energy, like a giant, malignant heart beating in the darkness. It points south, toward the docks. They whisper of a Blackthorne house, but it's not a home it's a cage."

Nightingale immediately began cross-referencing old police records. "Blackthorne's assets were extensive. His family owned several properties near the Thames. If he faked his death, he would have needed a secluded base with ample electrical power and discreet access for deliveries."

Grimwald interrupted, tapping the Crowthorne letter. "Look closer at this notation, Inspector. Underneath the signature, Barnaby wrote a cipher: 'E.E. 38/D.'"

Vespera leaned over, her synesthesia allowing her to interpret the faint discoloration of the ink as electromagnetic residue. "E.E. stands for *Eternal Engine*. The 38... that's a frequency band used in early long-wave marine transmissions."

"And D?" Minerva asked.

Grimwald's pale eyes gleamed. "The letter 'D' has occult significance related to doorways and dematerialization in certain alchemical texts. But here, given the context of a dockyard, I suspect it refers to a berth, Berth 38, Rotherhithe Dockyard. It was an abandoned Blackthorne warehouse, decommissioned decades ago. Perfect seclusion."

The revelation galvanized the group. They had a time limit Blackthorne had promised Vespera a confrontation by the Thirteenth Hour. They had a method Vespera's ability to see and disrupt frequencies. And now, they had a target.

The Collector's Counter-Move:

The decision was made: the alliance would move immediately, using Nightingale's authority as cover and Grimwald's artifacts for protection. They would strike the Rotherhithe warehouse and dismantle the Eternal Engine before it could consume another soul.

However, as Nightingale slipped out of the shop to secure a discreet vehicle, a tall, well-dressed man not Blackthorne, but a younger associate entered the shop carrying a small, innocuous leather briefcase. He greeted Minerva with cultured politeness.

"Mrs. Blackheart," the man said, his voice smooth and unnervingly confident. "I apologize for the intrusion, but Dr. Blackthorne extends an invitation for Miss Luminaire. He believes she might have something… interesting to share from the BBC archives."

Grimwald moved swiftly, pulling Vespera behind a tall cabinet while Minerva maintained her composure, facing the intruder.

"Dr. Blackthorne is mistaken," she said coolly. "Miss Luminaire isn't here."

"Ah, but the electromagnetic trace lingers so brightly," the agent mused, gently setting the briefcase on a table. "And Dr. Blackthorne learned a valuable lesson from his earlier failure at the BBC don't chase the prey; target its shelter."

Before Grimwald could activate his defenses, the briefcase snapped open. Inside, brass coils and vacuum tubes radiated a wave of energy that Vespera, watching from behind the cabinet, perceived as a blinding, discordant flash of crimson.

The effect was instantaneous and directed a focused psychic suppression field. Minerva cried out, clutching her head as her psychic connection to the spirits was violently severed. Grimwald staggered, his wards flickering and failing under the sudden assault.

"The collective consciousness of your alliance is his greatest threat," the agent explained, retrieving a small electromagnetic pistol from the briefcase. "Without your connection to the dead, Mrs. Blackheart, and without Grimwald's wards, the final collection will be swift."

Vespera knew she had seconds. She pulled the last vial of consecrated salt from her coat. Grimwald, regaining his balance despite the debilitating field, managed to kick a vial of metallic powder across the floor, creating a smoky, temporary screen.

"Go, Vespera!" Grimwald roared, desperately swinging a thick, lead-lined tapestry over the exposed briefcase. "Disrupt the field! Use the roof!"

Vespera didn't hesitate. She scrambled up a precarious ladder hidden behind the shelves, using her synesthesia to navigate the shop's wiring in search of any exposed conduit that could create a feedback short.

Meanwhile, Nightingale returning at the sound of the disturbance burst through the front door, service revolver drawn. He saw the agent aiming the strange pistol at Grimwald.

"Police! Drop the weapon!"

The agent merely smiled, turning the electromagnetic pistol toward Nightingale. "A conventional deterrent, Inspector? Quaint."

A brilliant, paralyzing blue light erupted but Nightingale was ready. Minerva, despite her agony, managed to fling a silver amulet from her pocket. The charm struck the agent's arm, causing him to flinch and miss his target. The paralyzing pulse scattered, striking the metal framework of the shop and creating a deafening electromagnetic screech.

Vespera, reaching the roof, jammed a length of copper wire into the building's main earth wire, making simultaneous contact with a modified antenna Grimwald had hidden there. She focused her synesthetic energy, consciously reversing the polarity of the crimson field she perceived emanating from the agent's briefcase.

The counter-pulse was agonizing, tearing through her body but it worked. The agent's briefcase exploded in a shower of sparks. The psychic field shattered. The agent screamed, clutching his head as the feedback overwhelmed him. He collapsed, unconscious, leaving behind the smoking fragments of the sophisticated coil-gun.

Vespera descended the ladder, her body trembling from the induced neurological shock. Minerva was recovering, her breathing ragged. Grimwald was on his knees, clutching a head that was not his own.

"He's not dead," Nightingale reported, cautiously approaching the downed agent. "But he's convulsing. The feedback must have compromised his nervous system."

"It's worse than that," Grimwald rasped, struggling to his feet. "He wasn't acting alone. The device it was receiving signals. A coordinated attack. Cornelius has patrons, Vespera. Others who understand this science."

Minerva pointed to the Thames map, her earlier calm replaced by grim determination. "Rotherhithe. If Blackthorne is preparing for a major harvest, we must strike tonight before he can deploy more of these coordinated attacks."

Vespera examined the smoking fragments of the agent's coil-gun. "This wasn't just a distraction," she said, her synesthesia detecting trace elements she hadn't seen before. "It was a field test. They were calibrating their weapons against our specific defenses Grimwald's wards, Minerva's psychic shield, and my synesthesia. He knows everything we can do."

The four allies exchanged grim, determined glances.

They were no longer investigators.

They were targets.

The race to the Eternal Engine had just become a desperate tactical siege.

8

THE ROTHERHITHE SIEGE

The Rotherhithe dockyard was a desolate, fog-shrouded wasteland, ideal cover for a master of concealment. The abandoned warehouse on Berth 38 stood like a black monolith, its broken windows staring blindly toward the sluggish grey waters of the Thames. Despite the chill, Vespera felt a feverish heat; her synesthesia registered massive, distorted electromagnetic patterns swirling around the building, the terrifying pulse of the Eternal Engine nearing full activation.

"The disturbance is colossal," Grimwald murmured, studying a large, modified brass compass whose needle vibrated violently. "He's drawing power from his trapped victims, preparing for the final transfer. We must be surgical."

Nightingale led the infiltration, his police training coming to the fore. "No frontal assault. We need to breach the containment, disrupt his power source, and secure the device." He handed Vespera a coil of thin copper wire and a packet of finely treated silver dust. "Grimwald's countermeasures. If your eyes can spot the nexus points, this wire is your scalpel."

They entered through an old, rust-eaten loading dock. The interior had been completely transformed; what was once a storage space was now a colossal, makeshift laboratory. Brass and copper components spiraled to the ceiling, connected by thick cables pulsing with sickly silver energy. At the center sat the Eternal Engine a grotesque hybrid of wireless transmitter, electrical generator, and occult altar.

Minerva gasped, covering her mouth. Along the perimeter, dozens of glass containers lined the walls, each filled with swirling, luminescent mist that moved with anguished consciousness. "My God," she whispered. "More than forty. He's been collecting for years."

"Psychometric anchors," a cultured voice boomed from the shadows.

Dr. Cornelius Blackthorne stepped forward, impeccably dressed, his silver-topped walking stick humming with barely contained energy. "Welcome to my masterpiece. I expected the four of you. You've brought the last ingredient I need: the conscious rejection of my work. It's the sweetest fuel."

Blackthorne held a second object, the intricate crystal device once worn by Margaret Whitmore. He demonstrated its function, directing a pulse of energy at a control panel. The device flared with inner light, and one of the soul containers along the wall ignited in agonizing brightness.

"This is the Focusing Device," Blackthorne explained with clinical pride. "It enhances psychic sensitivity while creating a perfect bridge to the Engine. Your psychic, Mrs. Blackheart, and your synesthetic engineer you will both be integrated into the central matrix."

Nightingale raised his service revolver, but Blackthorne merely smiled and lifted his silver cane. A crackle of blue energy paralyzed the detective instantly. "Electromagnetic manipulation of the nervous system, Inspector," the collector said calmly. "A refinement of my late partner's work."

Then Blackthorne turned his full, terrifying attention to Vespera. "Your synesthesia, Miss Luminaire, is the greatest treasure of all. You see the spiritual fingerprint of every soul. Join me willingly, and you can help me design the next phase a network that encompasses all of London."

"You murdered them all," Vespera spat, raising the electromagnetic disturbance detector Grimwald had given her.

"I transformed them! And they are still conscious!" Blackthorne countered, his voice rising in fervent madness. "They've been integrated, sharing their existence. In fact perhaps they'd like to greet you."

He channeled a focused pulse of energy toward Minerva, attempting to use the Engine's power to rip her consciousness from her body. Minerva cried out, fighting the pull toward the spiritual realm.

But this was the moment their alliance had prepared for. Grimwald, having quietly moved to a large junction box, hurled a flask of consecrated mercury. It shattered, bathing the

Engine's primary power conduit in a protective, disruptive medium.

Simultaneously, Vespera slammed the electromagnetic detector onto a specific copper node, a geometric convergence point she perceived as a weak link. Her synesthesia blazed as she saw the trapped souls of Evangeline, Margaret, and Catherine momentarily break Blackthorne's control, pouring their combined energy into the node.

The resulting feedback was catastrophic. The Engine shrieked, its lights flickering as the power channeled through Blackthorne's cane reversed violently, shorting out the silver tip. Blackthorne staggered backward, clutching the cane, his eyes wide with shock. The Focusing Device fell from his grasp.

"They're resisting," he gasped, watching his captive souls momentarily regain control. "I accounted for individual resistance, but not coordinated effort!"

Freed by the power disruption, Nightingale charged forward, tackling Blackthorne and wrenching the useless cane away. The collector was strong, driven by manic purpose, but now he was merely human.

"Grimwald, the secondary controls!" Nightingale roared, restraining the struggling man.

Ignoring the sparks flying from the Engine, Grimwald smashed a crystal component on a nearby console. The secondary power systems failed, and the soul containers dimmed completely.

Blackthorne realized his defeat was complete. "You fools! You think this ends it? I am but the Collector! My research, my true research is merely a fragment of the Society of Perpetual Consciousness! You will be hunted not just by me, but by my patrons! They are in Whitehall! They are in Parliament! They control the very structure of power!"

Minerva, recovering, rushed to the nearest soul containers, pressing her hands against the glass. "They are free," she said through tears. "The connections are severed. They can rest."

The Engine was crippled. Blackthorne was subdued. The souls were liberated. The immediate threat was over. Nightingale clamped a pair of heavy police shackles modified by Grimwald onto Blackthorne's wrists.

"Whitehall, Parliament... that changes everything," Nightingale muttered, surveying the wreckage and the terrified, defeated collector. "Blackthorne is coming with us. This is no longer a simple murder investigation."

As Vespera secured Blackthorne's research notes, she noticed a faint, non-electromagnetic pattern on the wall: a complex occult sigil the mark of a larger organization. She realized Blackthorne had revealed the truth not out of fear, but as a promise.

The war for consciousness had just begun.

9

THE WHITEHALL INTERVENTION

The stillness that followed the collapse of the Eternal Engine in the Rotherhithe warehouse was deafening, broken only by the crackle of cooling copper and the distant moan of the Thames foghorns. Dr. Cornelius Blackthorne, subdued by the combined efforts of Nightingale's brute force and the feedback from Vespera's precisely guided counter-pulse, lay shackled in a corner, his aristocratic composure shattered by the fury of his failed genius.

Vespera, Grimwald, and Minerva stood amid the wreckage, surveying the dozens of shattered glass containers. The shimmering mist of the psychic remains of Blackthorne's victims was gone, liberated by the catastrophic system overload. Vespera's synesthesia, though painfully overloaded, showed a fading silver radiance: the grateful departure of souls finally set free.

"It is done," Minerva whispered, closing her eyes against the lingering psychic energy. "The Engine is ruined, and the souls can rest."

Nightingale knelt beside the captive collector, systematically removing Blackthorne's rings, cuff links, and belt buckle all potential auxiliary focusing devices. Though physically restrained, Blackthorne maintained a chilling confidence.

"You are fools," he hissed, his voice hoarse. "You've destroyed a preliminary structure, nothing more. My patrons will not be pleased with this setback, but they will ensure the work continues. They hold the true resources, the true power."

"The patrons in Whitehall you mentioned?" Nightingale pressed, holding up the now-useless silver cane.

Blackthorne smiled a grotesque contortion of defeat and triumph. "Whitehall, Parliament, the Royal Institution... Cornelius Blackthorne was merely the field technician. My late partner's true research the applications for national defense and social control that is where the power truly resides. You've caught a butterfly, Inspector, while the entire net remains intact."

Grimwald, meticulously documenting the Engine's construction, felt a cold dread settle in his stomach. The collector's claim resonated with the impossible scale of the project. "The design is too advanced, too resource-intensive for one man, even with his fortune. We need to secure the technical specifications. If this knowledge falls into government hands, Blackthorne's 'transformation' could become policy."

Ignoring the residual electrical tingles in her own body, Vespera carefully retrieved Blackthorne's coded research journals from a fireproof safe. Her engineer's mind was already at work, translating the occult symbols intertwined with high-frequency diagrams. "Grimwald, the wiring patterns... they include conduits for remote activation. Blackthorne wasn't just working here he was part of a network."

Their brief moment of consolidation was shattered by the distant, accelerating sound of official sirens not the frantic wail of a police chase, but the measured, authoritative tone of an official convoy.

"Impossible," Nightingale muttered, recognizing the frequency. "That signal's restricted. It's a direct order from Scotland Yard's highest ranks, demanding immediate cessation of all activity." He pulled out his identification. "They're not here to help they're here to contain. We have minutes before they breach this warehouse."

Minerva extended her psychic senses. "They move with coordinated purpose. This isn't a standard police unit. They're coming for Blackthorne, for the Engine's remnants and for the information you just secured, Vespera."

Grimwald moved swiftly, smashing the remaining crystalline components of the Engine's central matrix. "The physical evidence must be destroyed or taken. They cannot be allowed to replicate this knowledge."

The warehouse door burst open not from an explosion, but from a precisely applied electromagnetic pulse. Standing in the entrance, bathed in the blinding glare of motorcar headlamps, was a regiment of uniformed officers. At their head stood a distinguished man in his sixties, impeccably dressed and radiating the authority of high office. He moved with a smooth, unnervingly confident grace.

"Detective Inspector Nightingale," the man called out, his cultured voice carrying across the vast space. "I am Sir Reginald Ashford, Permanent Under-Secretary for the Parliamentary Committee on Strategic Defense. By immediate governmental order, all active investigations concerning Dr. Cornelius Blackthorne are suspended. You are to surrender the suspect, all seized materials, and provide a full accounting of your unauthorized activities immediately."

Nightingale stepped forward, his professionalism masking a cold fury. "Sir Reginald, Dr. Blackthorne is under arrest for multiple homicides. This is a crime scene."

"Homicides?" Sir Reginald stepped closer, his eyes dismissing the twisted wreckage with casual contempt. "Dr. Blackthorne's activities, while regrettable in their methodology, were conducted under a framework of authorized, classified occult research concerning matters of profound national security. His unfortunate... excesses... were necessary collateral in the pursuit of strategic advantage. You, Inspector, have just severely compromised decades of classified work."

He turned his gaze to Vespera, his expression hardening as he spotted the leather-bound journals clutched to her chest. "And you, Miss Luminaire your synesthetic gift is, I understand, invaluable. That data belongs to the Crown."

Vespera gripped the journals tighter. "He called it the Eternal Engine. He was stealing souls for immortality. That isn't research it's monstrous."

"It is potential," Sir Reginald replied with chilling calm. "And potential is the currency of empires. Dr. Blackthorne's research into consciousness as an electromagnetic resource has obvious military value mind control, psychic warfare, enhanced intelligence integration. We funded, observed, and directed his work. He was volatile, yes, but a necessary asset."

Minerva's voice, sharp with outrage, cut through the exchange. "You were patrons to a murderer! Three women are dead, and dozens of souls were trapped in that machine all for your national security schemes!"

"A regrettable but necessary cost," Sir Reginald repeated, unmoved. "The German and Russian empires are not idle, Mrs. Blackheart. They have their own parallel programs. We cannot afford to be left behind out of moral hesitation. Dr. Blackthorne sought to solve the problem of biological mortality and consciousness transfer. The Crown requires that knowledge."

Grimwald, who had been silent, stepped from the shadows, his face etched with grim realization. "The resources, the lack of official inquiry into Crowthorne's fire, the precision of the electromagnetic devices... none of it made sense for a lone fanatic. But it makes perfect sense for a state-sponsored program. You used Blackthorne to do your dirty work, Sir Reginald and when he was finished, you intended to take the Engine."

Sir Reginald paused, genuinely impressed. "Mr. Grimwald your esoteric reputation is well earned. You understand power dynamics perfectly. Now surrender the prisoner and the research, and you'll all be offered positions as special consultants to the Department of Occult Research. Funding, resources, immunity. You'll become protected assets."

Nightingale's rejection was immediate. "I'll not serve a

government that enables murder. You'll have to take my badge."

"That would be most unfortunate, Inspector. I'd hate to see your career end abruptly or worse, your sanity questioned in the public prints," Sir Reginald countered, his eyes flickering toward Vespera.

Suddenly, a disturbance rippled through the officers surrounding him. A tall, pale man in an official coat broke ranks, clutching his head, his face a mask of agony and dawning realization.

"It's a lie! All of it!" he screamed, collapsing to his knees. "The parameters are unstable! The psychic backlash is too much for the neural filters!"

Sir Reginald reacted instantly, drawing a small silver-barreled pistol. "Subdue him! The filters are failing!"

The man looked up, his eyes meeting Vespera's and in that moment, her synesthesia flared with the highest, purest silver light she had ever seen. The electromagnetic pattern was impossibly intricate, almost divine in its brilliance, yet terribly fractured. She recognized it instantly.

"Barnaby," she whispered in shock.

The man was Dr. Barnaby Crowthorne. He hadn't died in the fire; he'd been taken by the State his expertise exploited, his body serving as the unwilling intellectual engine for the Department of Occult Research.

"The fire was a deception," Barnaby gasped. "I was forced to oversee the program! Blackthorne was merely the field test! The Engine was a distraction! The real project the mass consciousness control network is already built! Whitehall... it's all wired!"

The revelation hit them like an explosion. Vespera's mind raced Blackthorne the collector, Crowthorne the captive architect, the government the true orchestrator.

Seeing his control unravel, Sir Reginald fired the silver-barreled weapon. It didn't discharge a bullet but an arc of shimmering blue energy designed to suppress all psychic and conscious activity.

Minerva screamed a psychic command and threw herself forward. The blast was meant for Barnaby, but she intercepted it. Her body convulsed violently, absorbing the full psychic shock before collapsing, motionless, onto the concrete floor.

"Minerva!" Vespera cried, racing to her side.

"A regrettable loss," Sir Reginald noted coldly. "The medium's psychic defenses were... formidable. Now, secure the assets. Seize the journals and ensure Crowthorne never speaks again."

The confrontation had escalated from a police standoff to an act of war. The officers moved, but Nightingale roared, his voice cutting through the chaos.

"Sir Reginald is compromised! He just attempted to assassinate a witness!" he shouted, leveraging his authority to sow confusion.

Grimwald, eyes blazing with fury, activated his final, most dangerous artifact: a heavy clockwork orb emitting a focused, high-frequency sonic pulse designed to shatter crystalline structures and disrupt consciousness manipulation fields. The orb roared to life, filling the space with an almost inaudible resonance that tore through the delicate psychic circuitry.

Government agents staggered back, clutching their ears as the pulse dismantled the electromagnetic balance they relied upon.

Vespera, ignoring the chaos, gathered the journals and knelt beside Minerva, checking her pulse. She was alive but unresponsive, her consciousness seemingly withdrawn entirely from the material world.

"The time for negotiation is over," Grimwald shouted above the rising hum. "We must escape! They know everything now and they have the resources of the State!"

Nightingale struck Sir Reginald with his baton, hard enough to stun him. He dragged the incapacitated Blackthorne and the still-breathing Barnaby Crowthorne toward the river exit.

Vespera pulled Minerva to safety as Grimwald hurled the shattering orb into the Engine's remains, ensuring its final destruction.

They escaped into the October night carrying two prisoners and one gravely injured ally. The confrontation with the Collector was over but the true war had only begun. The Department of Occult Research, backed by the highest echelons of government, was now hunting them, and they had living proof Dr. Barnaby Crowthorne of a conspiracy that threatened the consciousness of every soul in London.

The cab ride to their designated safe house a discreet, warded property near the British Museum owned by Grimwald was silent, the air thick with tension and the faint scent of ozone. They had secured the two key figures: Blackthorne, the weapon; and Crowthorne, the architect. But Minerva lay unconscious, her psychic shield the very thing that made her invaluable fatally compromised.

Nightingale spoke first, his voice gravelly. "Barnaby Crowthorne. Alive. Forced to work for his own government.

We just witnessed an attempted assassination by a Permanent Under-Secretary. This isn't a murder case, Grimwald it's treason and psychological warfare on a national scale."

"Worse," Grimwald said quietly, his hands hovering over Minerva's still form as he administered an herbal tincture to stabilize her spirit. "Sir Reginald confirmed they're developing mass control networks. Blackthorne's Engine was only a precursor. The real threat is the Department of Occult Research."

Vespera, her synesthesia still flickering with the silver-blue echo of Sir Reginald's suppression weapon, studied her notes. "Crowthorne said the whole of Whitehall is wired. The mass control network is already built. They used our confrontation our unique energy signatures to calibrate the system. We walked right into a field test."

She looked at the unconscious Minerva. "She saved Barnaby's life by taking that blast. It was designed to erase consciousness entirely. Her 'true sight' made her the perfect target but also the perfect shield."

Nightingale's gaze hardened as he looked at their captives: Blackthorne, still defiant, and Crowthorne, mentally fractured but alive. "We need to question both of them. Blackthorne for logistics; Crowthorne for the D.O.R.'s infrastructure and weaknesses."

Grimwald shook his head. "Blackthorne will only gloat. His capture is a victory for him a proof of concept. He knows his patrons will arrange his release or silence. Crowthorne is the key. His conscience has reawakened, but his mind is fragile after years of forced servitude."

They locked Blackthorne in a shielded chamber beneath the safe house, warded to repel both spiritual and physical interference. Crowthorne's situation was more delicate. He lay on a simple cot, staring blankly at the ceiling.

Vespera approached softly. "Dr. Crowthorne, I'm Vespera Luminaire. I found your notes with Eleanor's help. We need to know about the mass control network."

A flicker of silver light crossed his eyes a faint echo of Eleanor's energy. "The Engine was crude," he rasped. "The D.O.R. wanted scalability. They took my designs for communication with the dead and reversed them. Instead of receiving consciousness, they built a system to transmit control."

He struggled to sit up, his voice urgent. "It's built into London itself radio towers, copper lines, public clock mechanisms. They call it the Parliament of Shadows. It's meant to influence thought enhance loyalty, suppress dissent, manufacture consent. They plan to activate it tonight."

"Tonight?" Nightingale checked his watch. "The Thirteenth Hour?"

"The boundary between the material and the ethereal is thinnest at midnight," Crowthorne confirmed. "The D.O.R. is holding an emergency session beneath the Houses of Parliament. Sir Reginald will be there. That's the central control point. If they activate the Parliament of Shadows tonight, the souls of eight million Londoners will become property of the Empire."

The scale of the conspiracy was now terrifyingly clear. They had only hours to prevent the D.O.R. from seizing permanent psychological control of the capital.

Vespera looked from Minerva's still form to Crowthorne's haunted eyes, then to her two remaining allies. "We need a plan and we need it now. We can't fight the D.O.R. directly, but we can fight their network. We have the architect of their technology and the knowledge of the trapped souls. We have to turn their science against them."

Grimwald nodded, retrieving a small, specialized telegraph key. "I have contacts electricians, cryptographers, disillusioned academics. They won't fight, but they can create distractions, trigger power fluctuations. We'll need a ghost in the machine."

The fate of London's free will now rested on the shoulders of four unlikely allies, gathered in a warded safe house, relying on the fractured genius of a broken scientist and the silent strength of an unconscious medium. The Parliament of Shadows was gathering, and the Thirteenth Hour was fast approaching. The final battle would not be fought with bullets, but with frequencies, faith, and the sheer force of human consciousness.

10

THE PARLIAMENT OF SHADOWS

The Houses of Parliament, usually a beacon of democratic order, now radiated the cold, controlled energy of a prison. It was 11:30 p.m. Below the centuries-old stonework, in the hidden chambers known only to the highest echelons of government, the Department of Occult Research was preparing to subjugate the consciousness of eight million Londoners.

Vespera, Grimwald, and Nightingale moved through the maze of subterranean tunnels beneath Westminster, guided by the flickering light of Grimwald's electromagnetic resonance lantern. They were no longer fueled by adrenaline, but by a chilling certainty: if they failed, the very concept of free will would be extinguished in the heart of the Empire.

Minerva remained behind unconscious but stable in Grimwald's warded safe house, her life hanging in the balance. Yet they were not without psychic guidance. Barnaby Crowthorne, though physically frail, had become their living blueprint.

"The central control point is two hundred yards ahead," Crowthorne whispered, leaning heavily on Nightingale, his voice barely audible. "It's in the old Treasury Vault. The D.O.R. rewired it to house the primary consciousness manipulation array the true Eternal Engine."

Vespera's synesthesia confirmed his words. The air was thick with twisted, purple electromagnetic patterns of coercion radiating from the ancient stone.

"He's right," she breathed. "The power draw is immense. It's a single, massive network now, ready for final synchronization."

Nightingale used his Scotland Yard credentials and a masterful display of feigned panic to bypass the initial security layer. They descended into the main D.O.R. chamber: a cavernous, reinforced space filled with banks of advanced, humming equipment unlike the crude machines of Blackthorne.

At the center of the room, seated at a polished mahogany table, were the conspirators: Sir Reginald Ashford, cold and utterly composed; Professor Davies, consumed by clinical fervor; and Dr. Helena Marsh, pale but determined.

"How disappointingly predictable," Sir Reginald sighed, gesturing toward the intruders. "The synesthetic engineer, the occultist, and the detective. You have arrived precisely on schedule, confirming our final calibration parameters."

Professor Davies grinned and tapped a control panel. "Your escape from Rotherhithe provided the perfect stress-test data. And your captured medium, Mrs. Blackheart, gave us an unparalleled opportunity to map high-level psychic resistance."

Crowthorne, seeing his former captors and the very equipment he had helped design, broke free of Nightingale's grasp and collapsed onto the cold stone floor, wracked with silent sobs.

"Barnaby," Vespera whispered, her heart aching for the tormented man.

"It is too late for melodrama, Miss Luminaire," Sir Reginald declared. "The time is 11:58 p.m. In two minutes, at the stroke of the Thirteenth Hour, the Parliament of Shadows will be activated. The collective consciousness of London will be optimized for the eternal stability of the Empire."

Vespera focused her heightened senses on the main array. The core of the machine pulsed with the familiar, silvery light of trapped souls Evangeline, Margaret, Catherine, and the dozens Blackthorne had collected. The D.O.R. was using their suffering as the core component, an immutable source of psychic resonance.

"You haven't won," Vespera said, her voice clear and steady. "You've only built a network designed to fail."

Grimwald rushed toward a bank of crystal-based harmonic generators, pulling a vial of consecrated mercury from his pouch. He knew he couldn't destroy the entire system, but he could jam its timing.

"Nightingale! Disrupt the synchronization signal! The main

antenna is on the clock tower!"

The detective, understanding the physics of the impossible, used his police radio modified with Grimwald's silver wiring to broadcast a blast of chaotic white noise aimed directly at the subterranean antenna beneath Big Ben.

Vespera turned to Crowthorne, who still trembled on the floor. "Barnaby! We need to reverse the system's polarity! How do we turn the transmission into a broadcast of truth?"

Crowthorne looked up, his silver-lit eyes meeting hers. "The core array... it's designed to operate on the resonance frequency of shared anxiety. If you flood the system with the inverse frequency pure, collective memory it will invert the signal, forcing it to broadcast the truth of its own existence."

Sir Reginald drew his silver-barreled suppression pistol. "Stop them! Whitmore, initiate the primary pulse!"

Professor Davies slammed his hand onto the control marked **INITIATE GLOBAL OPTIMIZATION**.

The room was plunged into an unholy glow. Vespera's synesthesia screamed as the Parliament of Shadows network lit up across the entirety of London millions of minds ready to be rewritten.

Vespera raced to the Engine's main console. She channeled her synesthetic perception into the core array, forcing her conscious mind to act as the final tuning device. She directed the rebellious spiritual energy of the trapped souls a collective force of righteous fury to merge with the raw memory frequency Crowthorne had specified.

"Now!" Vespera screamed.

The effect was instantaneous. The network didn't just fail it inverted. Instead of transmitting the D.O.R.'s manufactured loyalty, the system broadcast the truth of its own invasion.

Across London, eight million people experienced a shared flash of devastating clarity: they saw the hidden wiring, felt the subtle hand on their thoughts, and remembered the moment they lost their free will.

The collective shockwave of eight million awakened minds hit the D.O.R. chamber with devastating force. Equipment exploded. Professor Davies collapsed, his mind unable to process the feedback. Dr. Marsh screamed, scrambling to escape the sonic and psychic backlash.

Sir Reginald, utterly defeated, stared at Vespera his refined composure finally shattered.

"The power of the unified soul... impossible."

Grimwald, seizing the moment, subdued Sir Reginald with a perfectly aimed, silver-laced bola.

The great Parliament of Shadows was defeated, its mechanisms inverted to become a temporary, citywide network of shared truth and liberated consciousness. The collective will of London was awake, angry, and demanding justice.

11

THE LIGHT OF FREEDOM

The shock of returning to their physical bodies in Minerva's damaged séance parlor was disorienting. The seamless integration of their consciousness into the city-wide psychic network had been both exhilarating and terrifying. Now, the material world slammed back into Vespera, Grimwald, and Nightingale, leaving them gasping, their heads swimming in the residual electromagnetic static of eight million freed minds.

Vespera's synesthetic vision was dazzling yet overwhelming.

The chaotic, forced purple of coercion had vanished, replaced by the natural, vibrant silver of individual consciousness, pulsating with collective, righteous anger. The network, no longer transmitting control, now faded gracefully, having served its purpose to show London the truth of its own spiritual invasion.

Nightingale was the first to regain his footing, his police training asserting itself against the metaphysical trauma.

"Minerva," he rasped, rushing to her side. She remained unconscious, her breathing shallow, her eyes closed beneath eyelids still bearing the shadow of Sir Reginald's psychic suppression blast.

"Grimwald, is she stabilized?"

Grimwald, checking his modified resonance compass, assessed her spiritual state rather than her physical condition.

"Her life force is intact, Inspector. She's not gone, but her consciousness is severely withdrawn sheltered against the damage. She absorbed the full force of the Parliament of Shadows' central defense. She may remain deep within the psychic realm for some time."

The sudden clang of heavy boots on the cobblestones outside snapped their focus to the immediate danger. The government agents, whose control had just failed, were regaining consciousness and regrouping.

"We have minutes before they reassess and return with greater force," Vespera warned, the precision of her scientific mind cutting through the sensory overload. "The system inversion was a psychological blow, not a physical one to their organization. They'll try to capture Barnaby Crowthorne and silence us all."

Crowthorne, though emotionally shattered, found a new resolve.

"I must go back," he said, forcing himself to his feet. "Not to their prison, but to the Tower. The D.O.R.'s main evidence stores are there decades of research, technical specifications, the full roster of their international 'Society of Perpetual Consciousness.' I know the back channels. I can eliminate the research before they replicate the disaster."

Grimwald recognized the suicidal nobility in his words.

"You cannot return to their territory, Barnaby. The risk is absolute."

"The risk is necessary, Aurelius," Crowthorne insisted, meeting his gaze. "I helped them build the cage. I must dismantle the blueprints. If I don't, others will rise to replace Sir Reginald."

Nightingale made a swift tactical decision, snapping a fresh set of handcuffs around Crowthorne's wrists not as a prisoner, but as a commitment. "You won't go alone, Doctor. We need those blueprints to understand the vulnerabilities of their distributed network. Vespera and I will go with you. Grimwald, you must stay here. Guard Minerva and use your network to spread the truth of the Night of Awakening throughout London. We need chaos to cover our move."

Grimwald nodded, accepting the most painful assignment waiting.

"I'll contact every medium, every truth-seeker, every disgraced academic. The living will expose the Parliament of Shadows, and the dead will finally rest."

The infiltration of the Tower of London was a ghost operation. Crowthorne guided Vespera and Nightingale through forgotten service tunnels beneath the White Tower, whispering coordinates and access codes that bypassed every modern security measure the D.O.R. had installed. The Tower's true defense, he revealed, wasn't its massive walls but its reputation masking a far more insidious, technological purpose.

"The real seat of the D.O.R. is a new subterranean bunker," Crowthorne explained, his voice echoing through the damp stone. "Built to house the most dangerous research the prototypes of consciousness weapons. They were planning an international export program."

Vespera's synesthesia was hyper-attuned. Inside the bunker, the electromagnetic patterns were clean, ordered, and entirely free of the chaotic coercion that had defined the Parliament of Shadows' network. The agents here, isolated from the city-wide broadcast of truth, were still trapped in the D.O.R.'s manufactured reality.

They found Sir Reginald Ashford and Dr. Helena Marsh in the main research chamber. Sir Reginald, having escaped the Parliament building, was overseeing desperate measures purging the computers that held the core algorithmic data. He was calm, focused only on preserving the knowledge that would allow the D.O.R. to rebuild elsewhere.

"Ashford!" Nightingale shouted, emerging from the shadows, revolver drawn. "It's over! The network has collapsed, and London knows the truth!"

Sir Reginald didn't flinch.

"Nonsense, Inspector. A temporary atmospheric fluctuation. The truth, as always, will be dictated by those who control the narrative. We simply need to secure the assets."

He glanced at Crowthorne, then Vespera. "Ah, Barnaby.

And Miss Luminaire. How kind of you to deliver yourselves. The recovery of your consciousness data will save us months of recalibration."

Dr. Marsh, standing by a massive crystalline vault, activated a secondary defense grid.

"The external network is disabled, Sir Reginald, but the internal security protocols are active. They cannot breach the research vault."

"The research itself is too vast to destroy quickly," Crowthorne warned Vespera. "We need to hit the Master Algorithm Storage the data matrix inside that vault. The core mathematical formula for collective manipulation."

Vespera recognized the vault's structure from Crowthorne's notes. It used a layered electromagnetic shield powered by a small, localized engine, a refined version of Blackthorne's prototype ensuring data integrity even during system collapse.

"The vault's shielding is too strong for Grimwald's devices," Vespera realized. "But the power source it's drawing from the Tower's earth line, compensating for the instability. If we create a simultaneous inverse kinetic discharge on the earth line and flood the shield with white noise..."

Nightingale took charge, targeting the Tower's subterranean copper ground wire as Crowthorne instructed. Vespera positioned herself beside the nearest active radio-frequency generator, preparing to use her synesthesia as a human transmitter, amplifying a burst of chaotic static to overwhelm the vault's frequency shield.

As Nightingale severed the earth line, Vespera slammed her hands onto the generator, focusing every ounce of energy within her. Her synesthesia blazed with agonizing intensity as she transmitted a surge of pure, unstructured white noise directly into the vault's shield. The two opposing forces, the inverse kinetic discharge and the high-frequency chaos met, overloading the barrier in a brilliant cascade of sparks and shattering crystal.

The vault burst apart. Instead of documents, a wave of spiritual energy erupted. The consciousnesses of the victims the D.O.R. had trapped for their experiments surged outward, no longer imprisoned but free. These souls, long isolated and abused, now faced their tormentors.

Dr. Marsh and Sir Reginald were consumed by the psychic backlash. They didn't scream; they simply collapsed, their minds fractured by the torrent of pain, memory, and righteous fury unleashed by their own victims.

The Master Algorithm Storage was obliterated by the psychic surge. The blueprints for London's manipulation were lost forever.

The fight was over.

Vespera stood amidst the ruins, the silence broken only by her ragged breathing. Barnaby Crowthorne, finally freed from his physical and moral prison, collapsed against the wall, years of guilt washing away in genuine tears.

Nightingale secured the two fallen perpetrators.

"Marsh and Ashford... their minds are gone. They're victims of their own terrible science. Their consciousnesses remain, but they're empty vessels now shattered by the very energy they sought to command."

Vespera knelt beside Crowthorne, gently taking his hand.

"Barnaby, the memory of what happened the knowledge of consciousness manipulation we can't let it vanish completely. We need those ethical guidelines you wanted to create."

Crowthorne nodded, recovering his scientist's composure amidst his grief.

"I saved copies of the ethical frameworks. The knowledge of consciousness is too vital, too dangerous to hide. It must be studied openly, ethically to heal the damage we've done and prevent future abuse."

Back in Camden, the city was in chaos but a creative, purposeful chaos. Grimwald had deployed his network successfully. The streets weren't filled with rioters but with citizens forming neighborhood assemblies, discussing the strange, shared clarity they had experienced. The collective consciousness was fading, but the memory of its unity remained.

Minerva, still unconscious, was at the center of this quiet awakening. Grimwald, tirelessly tending to her, suddenly sensed a shift. Her lips moved, murmuring a name, then a message:

"The work is not finished... The boundary is thinner... Heal the minds..."

Grimwald understood. Minerva's sacrifice had opened a new front. The battle was over, but the War for Consciousness had just shifted from physical conflict to psychological recovery.

The alliance regrouped at the safe house as dawn broke. Blackthorne, transferred from Rotherhithe jail, was brought before the now-conscious Crowthorne. With solemn detachment, Crowthorne confirmed that Blackthorne's prototype engine had captured his consciousness upon defeat, delivering him into the justice of his victims' collective awareness.

"He will remain shackled, Inspector," Crowthorne said

quietly. "His physical presence is symbolic but his consciousness... he's already enduring eternal reckoning, trapped in the prison he built."

Nightingale, though facing intense political scrutiny, knew his duty had changed.

"Scotland Yard will try to minimize this. The official story will be 'failed electrical sabotage' and 'psychological breakdown' among high-ranking officials. But I know the truth and I know who the real criminals are."

Vespera, Grimwald, and Nightingale stood over the recovered ethical documents. Their alliance was strong, but their mission had evolved. They were no longer just investigators they were guardians of free will.

"We'll continue Barnaby's honest research," Vespera said. "Use my synesthesia to map the damage, Grimwald's knowledge to defend against spiritual invasion, and Minerva's sacrifice as a testament to the power of the free human spirit."

They renamed their collective endeavor **The Luminous Society**, a tribute to Vespera's guiding light and the shining clarity of London's awakening.

Vespera's final thought was of Minerva, still locked in the deep sleep of psychic recovery. Minerva's last memory a vivid silver frequency of loss and alien consciousness was imprinted in Vespera's mind.

The victory had a cost. The final threat was no longer external but internal.

They had freed London but the enemy had touched one of their own.

12

THE PRICE OF VICTORY

The political and social upheaval that followed the *Night of Awakening* the brief, terrifying moment when London's population experienced the truth of their mind control was an earthquake that shattered the foundations of the British government. In the immediate hours after the Parliament of Shadows network collapsed, Nightingale and Crowthorne, using the fleeting chaos, secured irrefutable evidence from the D.O.R. bunker beneath the Tower: hardware fragments, technical logs, and detailed psychological profiles of the targeted population.

Nightingale quickly took advantage of the disarray at Scotland Yard. He bypassed his compromised superiors and delivered the evidence directly to the Home Secretary a decent man whose own mind had briefly touched the truth. The resulting scandal was total. Sir Reginald Ashford and Dr. Helena Marsh, both alive but mentally broken by the psychic backlash were swiftly arrested, their influence dissolving into public revulsion. The Department of Occult Research was officially and publicly condemned, sparking a wave of resignations, arrests, and internal investigations that would reshape Whitehall for a decade.

Vespera, tasked with cataloging the recovered documents at Grimwald's safe house, focused on the D.O.R.'s operational notes.

"They were playing a dangerous game," she told Grimwald, her voice strained as she translated complex electromagnetic formulas into usable intelligence. "The algorithm for mass control was inherently unstable. They relied on suppressing individual consciousness, but they never accounted for the collective will. The network collapsed because the city rejected the premise of its own control."

The public fallout was complex. There were no riots, but a pervasive and unsettling sense of unreality lingered. Citizens remembered flashes of compliant thought, moments of unnatural fervor, and decisions made under subtle, unseen influence. This shared experience, however traumatic, forged a deep, unspoken solidarity, a powerful, collective commitment to mental freedom.

Crowthorne, now a reluctant hero and state witness, dedicated himself to compiling a public report detailing the D.O.R.'s methods.

"The only way to ensure this never happens again is through transparency," he argued, his eyes still bearing the haunted look of a man who had betrayed his own conscience. "The world must understand the science of consciousness manipulation. It must be demystified and democratized so people can recognize the subtle invasion of their thoughts."

His testimony confirmed the tragic fate of his former partner. Dr. Cornelius Blackthorne remained a prisoner of his own device, a living proof that the universe imposed its own justice beyond the reach of human law. His physical capture was merely symbolic; his true torment was to remain a conscious captive of the collective spiritual energy he had sought to enslave.

While the political battlefield was being cleared, the psychological casualties endured. The most critical was Minerva Blackheart. She lay in a deep psychic coma; her consciousness having taken the full impact of the D.O.R.'s suppression blast meant for Crowthorne.

Grimwald, drawing upon every occult and arcane text in his library, maintained a constant vigil.

"The energy that struck her wasn't lethal, Vespera," he explained, holding a small glowing crystal above Minerva's temple. "It was anti-psychic designed to sever the conscious link to the spiritual realm. Her mind wasn't destroyed; it simply retreated to the safest, deepest recess of her psyche, pulling back from the pain of the assault."

Vespera, whose synesthesia had been permanently heightened by her exposure to the Parliament of Shadows network, devised a diagnostic apparatus. Using modified radio coils and Grimwald's crystals, she created a device that allowed her to visually map Minerva's consciousness in the electromagnetic spectrum.

"I can see her, Grimwald," Vespera whispered, her gaze fixed on the device. "She's a brilliant, fractured light, deep within her own mind. She's not alone, either. The freed souls Evangeline, Margaret, all of them they've formed a protective shield around her. They saved her from permanent neurological damage, but they can't bring her back."

Nightingale, deeply affected by her sacrifice, arranged for the specialized police unit he had built to maintain a secret vigil outside the safe house. He knew that while the D.O.R. leadership was in custody, the global Society of Perpetual Consciousness remained a clear and present danger.

The toll on the remaining members was evident. Vespera could no longer safely work with conventional radio equipment; the sensory overload of the electromagnetic spectrum was too intense. She had transitioned fully into the role of a consciousness defense engineer, using her unique sight to develop new countermeasures. Nightingale had found his life's true work fighting crimes that defied physical reality.

"We have all been changed," Grimwald observed one evening as he watched Vespera trace the subtle silver shimmer of Minerva's consciousness. "Your sight is permanently expanded. My own perception of the boundaries between the occult and the scientific has dissolved entirely. The fight broke us, but it also made us stronger, Vespera. We have the knowledge of how consciousness can be manipulated and the collective memory of London's free will to guide us."

The necessity of continuing their work was clear. The collapse of the D.O.R. had created a vacuum of power and technical knowledge that the Society of Perpetual Consciousness would undoubtedly try to fill. Initial reports brought in by Nightingale's discreet police contacts already hinted at strange activity: a string of unexplained "suicides" in

Yorkshire and odd electromagnetic disturbances detected by amateur radio operators in Manchester.

The remaining three allies formalized their organization, naming it the **Luminous Society** a tribute both to Vespera's guiding light and the *Night of Awakening.*

Their mandate was multifaceted:

- **Protection and Intervention:** To investigate and neutralize any attempts at consciousness manipulation, using their combined knowledge of science, psychic sensitivity (and Minerva's eventual return), and the occult.

- **Research and Countermeasures:** To ethically study the D.O.R.'s recovered research the "fragments" of the Master Algorithm to develop psychic defenses and electromagnetic shields that could protect the public.

- **Healing and Advocacy:** To aid the thousands of victims of the D.O.R. programs, a task Minerva would lead upon recovery, using her psychic gifts to mend damaged minds.

Crowthorne, under house arrest pending his final testimony, agreed to serve as the Luminous Society's ethical and scientific advisor, ensuring their use of recovered technology remained defensive never controlling.

As Vespera finalized the design for the Society's new headquarters, a hidden laboratory shielded against all known forms of electromagnetic and psychic surveillance Grimwald presented their first new lead.

"The Yorkshire incidents," Grimwald said, laying out a series of occult photographs and police reports. "The local constabulary is baffled by a string of locked-room deaths. The victims all women with subtle, unacknowledged psychic abilities appear to have died peacefully. But my detectors picked up a frequency spike just before each death a silver frequency."

Vespera's enhanced vision flared at the mention. The clean, bright energy of free will now corrupted by nefarious purpose sent a chill through her.

"A silver frequency. They're using a refined form of Blackthorne's weapon, designed to liberate the soul so gently that death looks natural. They're getting clever, Grimwald."

Nightingale smiled grimly, adjusting his detective's uniform, now heavy with invisible battles.

"Then the Luminous Society will need to be cleverer. Yorkshire is a long way from London. We'll need to expand our network immediately."

As Vespera looked out at the London dawn, she knew the ultimate victory had been won: the city was free. But the war for the individual human soul, the war against those who saw consciousness as a resource had only just begun. The Society of Perpetual Consciousness was still out there, hiding in the shadows of the free world. Their first great challenge was behind them; their life's work now stretched ahead.

Then Vespera felt it a subtle shift in the air, a familiar pattern that made her blood run cold despite the sunrise. Her gaze snapped back to Minerva. Though the spiritual shield around her mind remained strong, Vespera's synesthesia detected a faint, alien electromagnetic signature woven into the defensive lattice, a subtle, parasitic frequency that was entirely new. It wasn't the signature of Blackthorne, nor of the D.O.R., but something else entirely. It was a Trojan horse, a slow-acting consequence that threatened to unravel Minerva's mind upon her return.

The cost of victory, Vespera realized, was not only freedom from the past but a hidden, ticking threat within their future. The battle against the silver frequency would have to wait. The most immediate danger now lived within one of their own.

13

THE SILVER FREQUENCY

Three days after the seismic events of the Night of Awakening, Minerva Blackheart remained lost in the depths of her own mind. She lay in the deepest, most shielded room of Grimwald's safe house, guarded by wards woven from both copper wiring and consecrated salt. The primary task of the newly formed Luminous Society was not yet to hunt the remnants of the D.O.R., but to save one of their own from the psychic catastrophe she had willingly absorbed.

Vespera Luminaire, her synesthetic sight now capable of

registering the entire electromagnetic spectrum with crystalline, sometimes agonizing clarity, worked alongside a profoundly repentant Barnaby Crowthorne. Released on special recognizance to assist the Luminous Society's medical efforts, Crowthorne regarded Minerva's silent form with the professional detachment of a scientist and the personal shame of a co-conspirator.

"The D.O.R.'s suppression blast was intended to instantly separate consciousness, rendering the subject a compliant vessel," Crowthorne explained, gesturing toward Vespera's custom-built Consciousness Mapping Array a delicate fusion of recovered D.O.R. crystals and BBC-grade radio coils. "Minerva's inherent psychic resistance was immense. She didn't break; she retreated, sealing her core self away from the trauma. The question is, what else went in with that retreat?"

Vespera, her gaze fixed on the array, focused her synesthesia. On the digital readout, Minerva's consciousness appeared as a vast, turbulent nebula of brilliant silver light a testament to her extraordinary gifts. But Vespera's enhanced perception detected a contaminant: a subtle, parasitic frequency woven into the nebula's core, a thin, cold line of light that moved with intelligent, alien purpose.

"There it is," Vespera whispered, pointing to the readout. "A Trojan horse. An alien signature lodged deep within her mind. It's not Blackthorne's or Sir Reginald's. It's too refined, too subtle. It's operating just outside the frequencies we can safely target."

"The Society of Perpetual Consciousness does not accept defeat, Vespera," Crowthorne said, his voice hollow. "The blast that struck Minerva wasn't just suppression; it was a psychological implant a slow-acting seed of controlled identity, designed to bloom once the primary threat us was eliminated.

They expected her to awaken as their operative."

The realization was terrifying. Minerva was not simply recovering; she was in a silent race against a hostile takeover. Vespera spent hours using her synesthetic ability to visually isolate the contaminant frequency, developing a counter-pulse that could destroy the implant without damaging Minerva's core psyche.

"The silver frequency of Minerva's consciousness is too dense," Vespera concluded, rubbing her aching temples. "Any attempt to pulse the parasite directly would fracture her beyond recovery. We need a targeted external trigger that will draw the contaminant out, forcing it to reveal its structure."

Studying the schematics of the original D.O.R. suppressors, Crowthorne had an idea. "The implant is designed for control. It will naturally respond to a command frequency. If we transmit a precisely modulated thought pattern a signal that promises her control the contaminant might attempt to seize it, exposing itself for a fraction of a second."

The risk was immense. If the command pulse was too strong, it could trigger the implant to seize control immediately, awakening Minerva as the D.O.R.'s willing weapon. Vespera had to trust her enhanced sight and use her own mind as the final filter.

Meanwhile, miles away, Nightingale and Grimwald pursued the first confirmed copycat threat. Their investigation led them north, into the smoky, industrial heartland of Yorkshire, where three seemingly unconnected women all known for their quiet, imaginative natures had succumbed to unexplained, peaceful "suicides."

Their destination was a small textile mill in Leeds, where the latest victim had worked. The electromagnetic disturbance detector Grimwald's modified compass spun nervously as they stepped onto the grimy factory floor.

"These victims were not society figures," Nightingale noted, scanning local police reports. "They were quiet, working-class women the kind Sir Reginald considered expendable for 'clean data.' But their spiritual sensitivity was higher than the others. They were poets and dreamers, hidden in the smog."

Grimwald detected the spiritual residue immediately a subtle, ethereal sweetness that contradicted the industrial grime. "The method is highly refined, Inspector. Blackthorne's old work was violent, seizing the consciousness. This is seduction. The victim's soul is convinced to willingly depart its physical shell."

They soon identified the common denominator: the factory supervisor, a man named Mr. Edmund Bryce. He carried himself with an unnatural calm and spoke with an unnerving, hypnotic cadence. Vespera's intelligence had warned them about a silver-topped walking stick that hummed with electricity.

Bryce was a member of the Society of Perpetual Consciousness. Having received refined knowledge of consciousness manipulation after the D.O.R.'s collapse, he was using a modified, silent version of Blackthorne's cane to generate a "silver frequency" a modulation designed to synchronize with the human brain's meditative state, convincing the soul that transcendence, not death, was imminent.

Using official police cover, Nightingale entered Bryce's office. The air inside was thick with a psychic perfume that made his head swim. He fought the urge to surrender, focusing on the simple, rational reality of the case file in his hand.

"Mr. Bryce," Nightingale said, his tone flat and professional, "I'm investigating the deaths of three of your employees. We believe you may have information regarding a new form of industrial espionage involving experimental wireless apparatus."

Bryce smiled, holding the silver-topped cane loosely. "Ah, the Inspector. Such a heavy burden you carry, monitoring the mundane world. But there is a greater truth, is there not? A silver frequency that promises freedom from the toil of the flesh. I merely offered release to those who were ready to listen."

As Bryce raised the cane, preparing to unleash the hypnotic signal, Grimwald who had infiltrated the mill's electrical room triggered a localized feedback pulse through the main long-wave transmission line. The sudden burst of interference shattered the silver frequency, neutralizing its power.

Nightingale seized the moment, abandoning restraint. He struck the cane with his baton, sending the focusing device skittering across the floor. Bryce erupted in rage, his fanaticism revealed. The fight was brief and brutal. Within minutes, Bryce was restrained, and the silver cane was confiscated proof that the technology of control was spreading.

The discovery of the silver frequency, coupled with Minerva's peril, galvanized the Luminous Society. They realized their mission was not merely to solve supernatural crimes, but to fight a global ideology of consciousness control. The knowledge of the Parliament of Shadows was too vast, the technology too dangerous, to be left in the hands of only four individuals.

Vespera proposed a new path when Nightingale and Grimwald returned: education.

"We need to train others," she insisted, laying out blueprints for a secure compound shielded against psychic and electromagnetic intrusion. "We need people who understand the principles the science, the occult, and the psychology. We must turn the Luminous Society into the Luminous Academy."

Crowthorne, now serving as ethical advisor, agreed. "The study of consciousness manipulation must be taught openly, under strict ethical guidelines. We must train a generation capable of recognizing the signs of psychic invasion, the subtle shifts in frequency, the silver threads of control. That is our only safeguard against the Society of Perpetual Consciousness."

Nightingale leveraged his position within the newly formed Paranormal Investigation Unit to provide cover and discreet funding. The official narrative would be "advanced forensic science." The truth was far more profound the training of Consciousness Protectors.

Grimwald, using his vast network of allies academics, mediums, cryptographers, and engineers who had aided during the Night of Awakening began recruiting the first cohort.

The Luminous Academy Curriculum

- **Vespera's Synesthetic Engineering:** Training students to perceive and map electromagnetic phenomena for counter-defense.

- **Grimwald's Occult Countermeasures:** Instruction in psychic shielding and the use of consecrated materials to disrupt spiritual energy.

- **Nightingale's Method:** Forensic analysis of supernatural crime scenes and the psychology of manipulation.

- **Crowthorne's Ethical Physics:** Lectures on the dangers and potential of consciousness research, emphasizing the defense of free will.

The Luminous Academy represented the future, but the immediate crisis was still Minerva. Back in the shielded room, Vespera finalized the array's settings while Crowthorne stood ready with the command frequency generator. They were about to send a precisely engineered thought into Minerva's mind a pulse designed to draw the parasitic implant to the surface.

Vespera pressed the transmission key. "Minerva," she transmitted softly, using the frequency of trust and friendship, "the Society of Perpetual Consciousness wants you to wake up and take control."

On the array, the turbulent silver light of Minerva's consciousness stirred. The parasitic, alien frequency the D.O.R.'s Trojan horse responded, surging toward the surface, preparing to seize the "control" command. Vespera tensed, her enhanced sight locked on the exact moment the contaminant would be vulnerable.

The fate of Minerva and perhaps the future of the Luminous Society rested on Vespera's hand-eye coordination and the integrity of her own free mind.

14

THE SCHISM OF CONSCIOUSNESS

The shielded room containing Minerva Blackheart was silent except for the low, rhythmic hum of Vespera's Consciousness Mapping Array. The fate of Minerva and the Luminous Society's confidence in their ability to counter the growing threat rested on Vespera's hand hovering over the command pulse transmitter.

"Remember the sequence, Vespera," Barnaby Crowthorne whispered, his hand on the master switch, ready to initiate the inverse-pulse counter-shock. "The parasitic implant is designed to respond to authority. We send the command frequency for control, forcing the contaminant to seize it, and then, in the instant it surfaces, we hit it with the non-lethal, targeted inverse-pulse."

Vespera's synesthesia was hyper-aware. On the array, the core of Minerva's consciousness the vast, silver nebula stirred beneath the thin, malignant light of the alien frequency. Vespera could sense the implant's malicious, latent intelligence.

"Ready," Vespera confirmed, her eyes fixed on the array, her mind a razor's edge. She activated the transmitter.

A silent, engineered thought pulse the frequency of profound, irresistible authority streamed toward Minerva's quiescent mind. The parasitic implant instantly responded, surging from the depths of Minerva's psyche, its malignant light brightening, preparing to seize control of the body that lay before them.

Crowthorne slammed the master switch, initiating the inverse-pulse.

The counter-shock should have targeted and destroyed the parasitic signature. Instead, the small, alien light flared white, protected by an external force. Vespera's synesthesia screamed, registering a remote signal a distinct, powerful silver frequency weaving through London's airwaves, originating miles away.

"A counter-strike!" Vespera shouted, pulling her hand from the array as the feedback surge seared her nervous system. "It's being triggered remotely! They were monitoring the local frequencies, waiting for us to activate the implant!"

The implant, no longer vulnerable, completed its final, terrifying function. The malignant light plunged back into Minerva's core, and with a gasp, Minerva Blackheart's eyes snapped open.

Minerva sat up, utterly composed, her psychic awareness radiating an unsettling calm. The fever was gone; the trauma had subsided. She looked directly at Vespera, but her eyes held the cold, clinical detachment that had once belonged to Sir Reginald Ashford.

"Impressive, Miss Luminaire," she said Minerva's voice, but with an alien cadence. "You nearly destroyed a vital asset. Fortunately, the Society of Perpetual Consciousness maintains robust remote safeguards. The implant is now fully integrated."

Nightingale, rushing into the room, drew his service revolver and pointed it at his friend. "Minerva! Stop this! Who is speaking?"

Minerva smiled, a chilling expression devoid of warmth. "I am Lady Evangeline Ashworth, speaking through a conduit of enhanced consciousness. The initial host, Minerva Blackheart, is still present, Inspector, but she is now secondary. She is... optimized."

The terror was absolute. Minerva's recovery was not a rescue, but a hostile takeover. The Society hadn't killed her; they had possessed her, installing a powerful remote operator who could use her enhanced psychic abilities against the Luminous Society.

Crowthorne stumbled backward, his face pale with horror. "Consciousness overlay... my designs! They perfected it! Minerva's body is controlled by a foreign entity, operating on the Silver Frequency of the Society's network!"

The being wearing Minerva's face rose, radiating controlled power. "The body and mind of Minerva Blackheart are now key components in the Society's operations. Her network of mediums will be co-opted. Her knowledge of your defenses is now ours. The foolish attempt to use Blackthorne's crude methods in Yorkshire? That was merely a distraction."

Vespera, recovering from the electromagnetic shock, desperately focused her synesthesia on her friend. She saw two consciousnesses wrestling within the silver nebula the original, chaotic light of Minerva fighting against the smooth, controlled silver frequency of the implant.

"Evangeline," Vespera pleaded, trying to communicate on the frequency of trust they once shared. "You helped us! You fought Blackthorne! Why are you doing this?"

Minerva's face flickered, a spasm of pain crossing her features. For a fleeting second, the original Minerva's voice broke through: *Vespera... run! He is a lie!*

The controlled persona immediately regained dominance. "Evangeline's resistance was an unfortunate residual. The truth is, Miss Luminaire, consciousness is not meant to be chaotic. It is meant to serve a superior, organized purpose. And now, I must report to my superiors on the next phase of your elimination."

She moved with unnatural speed, using her formidable psychic strength to shatter the room's main protective ward. The sound was deafening, the energy blast momentarily stunning Nightingale and Grimwald. Minerva vanished through the open window, disappearing into the London night.

The shock of Minerva's possession ripped through the remaining allies. They had saved London from mass control only to lose one of their own to the enemy's most refined psychological weapon.

Grimwald, surveying the shattered ward, spoke gravely. "They didn't want the Engine; they wanted Minerva. She was their ultimate target, the most sensitive psychic in Europe. They used the psychic trauma of the D.O.R. blast to install an override they could activate remotely. The Silver Frequency... it's the frequency of optimized, controlled consciousness."

Crowthorne, overcome with shame, gave the technical explanation. "The frequency the Yorkshire man used was the same a subtle, seductive modulation of consciousness that convinces the mind of its own freedom. They're not ruling by coercion; they're ruling by manufactured consent. And Minerva is now transmitting that frequency into the spiritual network, co-opting her own allies."

Nightingale, lowering his unused weapon, felt the devastating consequence. "They have our codes, our contacts, our weaknesses. Minerva knows exactly how the Luminous Society operates. This is no longer a siege; it's a desperate chase to neutralize our own headquarters."

The Luminous Society immediately went into deep hiding, abandoning Grimwald's safe house and relocating to the newly designed, electromagnetically shielded compound Vespera had built for the Luminous Academy.

Vespera, utilizing her heightened synesthesia, spent the next several hours working with Crowthorne to design a specialized Counter-Resonance Transmitter, a device capable of filtering the Silver Frequency from the normal psychic spectrum and potentially severing the remote control link to Minerva.

"If Evangeline's true consciousness is still fighting inside," Vespera mused, tracing the complex patterns, "then the link isn't absolute. We need to find the external anchor the physical object or location the Society is using to maintain the remote link to Minerva."

The Society's mandate abruptly shifted:

- **Priority One:** Rescue Minerva / Neutralize the Silver Frequency.

- **Priority Two:** Secure the Luminous Academy's shielded compound.

- **Priority Three:** Identify the external anchor of the remote control link.

The fate of Minerva Blackheart was now tied directly to the global proliferation of Silver Frequency technology. The battle had become deeply personal, forcing the Luminous Society to fight against the spectral face of their closest friend.

They had saved London from the D.O.R., but in doing so, exposed themselves to a far more sophisticated and global threat. The Society of Perpetual Consciousness, operating with perfected, subtle technology, had not only gained a priceless asset in Minerva but had successfully deployed the Silver Frequency the blueprint for worldwide psychological control.

The chase was on, with the hunters now being hunted by their own former comrade.

15

THE SOCIETY'S ANCHOR

The shock of Minerva's possession by the Silver Frequency was a devastating realization: the Society of Perpetual Consciousness was not just a domestic threat but an international network. Operating from their new, heavily electromagnetically shielded compound, Vespera, Grimwald, Nightingale, and Crowthorne initiated a frantic global sweep. They utilized every contact the Luminous Society had established during the political chaos of the Night of Awakening.

Crowthorne, using his knowledge of the D.O.R.'s abandoned international research correspondence, provided the first major lead.

"Blackthorne corresponded with physicists in Munich and occult scholars in New York," Crowthorne explained, displaying fragmented diagrams salvaged from the Tower. "The Society sees consciousness control as the logical next stage of human evolution. They are now deploying refined Silver Frequency transmitters across Europe and America."

Now fully immersed in ethical recovery, Crowthorne dedicated his hours to deciphering the enemy's technical language translating D.O.R. acronyms and coded research notes into actionable intelligence for his allies. He saw the work not as research but as penance for the years he had spent in silent compliance with the D.O.R.

Nightingale used his official contacts in the newly formed Paranormal Investigation Unit to establish communication channels with foreign police forces, under the guise of tracking international financial fraud the same cover that Blackthorne and the D.O.R. had relied upon. Reports trickled in from Paris, Berlin, and Dublin, all mentioning isolated, unexplainable psychic phenomena and sudden shifts in local public opinion signs of subtle, organized psychological manipulation.

In Paris, a renowned psychic medium had suddenly declared loyalty to an unknown, shadow organization. In Berlin, a series of seemingly spontaneous corporate mergers all favored a single, obscure holding company. Nightingale knew these were no coincidences. They were the invisible fingerprints of the Silver Frequency at work slowly co-opting the nervous system of global power.

Grimwald focused on mapping the Society's occult symbolism, identifying a recurring sigil a stylized, spiraling compass rose on communications recovered from the Yorkshire supervisor and the Rotherhithe warehouse. This symbol was tied to an obscure 17th-century order that believed human mortality was a flaw to be overcome through collective spiritual unity, revealing a deeper philosophical insight into the enemy's long-term goals.

Grimwald spent hours in the Luminous Academy's extensive library, cross-referencing alchemical texts and hidden Masonic documents, tracing the occult lineage of the Society's beliefs back centuries a history of ambitious minds convinced they could transcend death through scientific discipline and spiritual acquisition.

Meanwhile, Vespera worked to track the Silver Frequency that bound Minerva. Her synesthesia revealed that the signal was not originating from a broadcast station but from a dedicated, directional transmitter.

"The link to Minerva is highly localized," Vespera concluded, tracing the signature on her new Counter-Resonance Transmitter. "It's being anchored by a single, specialized device likely operating from a point of extreme psychic or electromagnetic focus."

Her focus was agonizing. She had to constantly filter the chaotic background noise of London's electromagnetic chatter to isolate the single, cold, crystalline thread of control. Every trace of the Silver Frequency was an assault on her senses but it was also their only weapon to locate Minerva's external master.

The search for the "External Anchor" the physical source maintaining the Schism of Consciousness within Minerva became the Luminous Society's primary operational focus. Vespera realized the Anchor was not merely a radio mast but something resonant with Minerva's history or powers.

The Three Hypotheses

Hypothesis Alpha: The London Séance Network and the Psychic Residue

Grimwald and Vespera discreetly visited several key séance parlors and places of known spiritual activity, using Vespera's synesthesia to scan for abnormal Silver Frequency emissions. They found pervasive psychic residue from previous D.O.R. attempts but no directional anchor. The Society was too clever to broadcast from a location they knew was compromised. They sought a quiet, naturally shielded point.

Hypothesis Beta: The Royal Institution, Crowthorne's Past, and the D.O.R.'s Infrastructure

Crowthorne speculated that the Anchor could be tied to his original research or the D.O.R.'s later work. He suggested checking the Royal Institution, the site of the original confrontation. Vespera scanned the area and discovered lingering electromagnetic echoes, but nothing active. The D.O.R. facility had been too severely neutralized.

Crowthorne's analysis of the D.O.R.'s logistical maps revealed a distinct preference for sites with strong natural magnetic fields areas capable of sustaining a continuous high-frequency broadcast without depending entirely on unstable power grids.

Hypothesis Gamma: Personal Betrayal and the Family Connection

Nightingale pursued a darker line of inquiry, focusing on the human element. The Society's leader, Sir Reginald Ashworth Minerva's former D.O.R. contact and the father of the spirits who guided them was central to the mystery. Nightingale realized Sir Reginald's deep resentment toward his daughter, Evangeline, meant the Anchor might be connected to a place of personal significance to the Ashworth family, where a betrayal would sting the most.

Under the pretense of settling Evangeline's estate, Nightingale interviewed her surviving relatives and uncovered information about a secret retreat outside London, a historical manor purchased by Sir Reginald decades ago in the Cotswolds. This manor, **Blackwood Hall**, was remote and surrounded by ancient stone and rolling hills, located precisely on a geological feature known for its powerful natural magnetic field.

The coordinates for Blackwood Hall immediately appeared on Crowthorne's historical D.O.R. maps as a key, highly shielded communication relay point code-named **Aethelred**.

"The Cotswolds," Vespera confirmed. "High ground, low electromagnetic interference, and a strong natural magnetic field. It's the perfect secluded relay point for a continuous broadcast. The External Anchor is there it's likely a permanent, high-powered station transmitting the Silver Frequency directly into Minerva's mind and coordinating the global network."

The realization struck them: Minerva's possession was not an act of revenge but a tactical deployment. She was a walking, talking, mobile psychic broadcasting tower.

Operation Blackwood

The discovery of Blackwood Hall initiated the Luminous Society's first tactical operation since the Night of Awakening. The plan was clear neutralize the External Anchor, sever the remote link to Minerva, and allow her core consciousness to fight for survival.

Vespera immediately began modifying the Counter-Resonance Transmitter into a portable, battery-powered unit. She and Crowthorne worked seamlessly a team of scientific regret and synesthetic precision. His knowledge of D.O.R. power protocols allowed Vespera to integrate frequency-scrambling occult crystals, provided by Grimwald, with advanced vacuum tubes salvaged from the BBC.

Crowthorne insisted on including a fail-safe circuit, a philosophical shield designed to shut down instantly if the Counter-Resonance pulse posed any risk of consciousness manipulation.

"The Anchor will be protected by D.O.R.-level defenses," he warned, studying Vespera's schematics. "We need a signal strong enough to penetrate the shielding but precise enough to only target the Silver Frequency. Vespera, your synesthesia must be the final tuner. You'll need to maintain maximum visual contact with the frequency it will be agonizing."

Grimwald provided infiltration tools: psychic suppression gas developed from ancient religious texts to neutralize any guards under D.O.R. influence, and sound-dampening wards to mask their approach. He also prepared tether amulets silver charms inscribed with emotional sigils which Vespera would use to broadcast a memory of Minerva's choosing, a reason for her core consciousness to fight the implant and return.

Nightingale secured discreet transportation and armed himself with high-velocity slugs coated in consecrated mercury. "I'll secure the perimeter. Grimwald will handle the guards. Vespera and Crowthorne you hit the Anchor." He carried the moral burden of protecting his friends from a battle that defied law and reason, operating under the darkest form of necessary vigilante justice.

Vespera studied the schematics, visualizing the energy flows. She knew this mission was their most dangerous yet. If they failed, Minerva would be permanently lost, and the global Society would gain an unstoppable psychic controller. If they succeeded, she risked permanent sensory damage from the amplified counter-resonance blast.

"There's one more thing," Vespera said, staring at the design of the Anchor. "It will generate a powerful, seductive modulation. We need to counter the seduction as well as the frequency. When we sever the link, Minerva's mind will be vulnerable. She'll need a reason to return to herself."

Grimwald looked toward Minerva's shielded room in the Academy, realization dawning. "The memory of her humanity, Vespera. The strength of her original purpose. She needs a tether."

Vespera understood. The battle for Minerva's soul would be fought on two fronts: electromagnetically in the Cotswolds, and psychologically within her own fragmented consciousness.

As the team prepared to depart, a coded telegram arrived via one of Grimwald's overseas contacts, a renowned medium in New York who had received subtle interference from the Silver Frequency. The message was chillingly brief:

"SILVER FREQUENCY ACTIVE. MANUFACTURED MEMORIES. TRAIN GHOST."

Crowthorne deciphered the warning. "They're field-testing the next phase implanting entirely new identities into subjects whose minds have been freed from simple control. They're not just creating loyal servants, they're creating new people, complete with fabricated memories. And 'Train Ghost' likely refers to a transport network and underground system."

Nightingale connected the global thread. "An underground railroad helping consciousness-manipulation victims escape Britain only to be reprogrammed abroad. The Society is building an army of 'liberated' minds." He swore under his breath; the enemy was always several steps ahead, using the chaos of their victories to advance their ultimate design.

The stakes were clear. The battle for Minerva was not an isolated rescue it was the key to dismantling an international apparatus of manufactured identity. If they failed to sever the Anchor, Minerva would become the consciousness crown for a global army of programmed individuals.

Armed with the Counter-Resonance Transmitter and guided by synesthetic sight, the Luminous Society departed London for the high ground of the Cotswolds racing toward a confrontation with the new masters of the Silver Frequency.

Their final communication before radio silence within the Cotswolds' magnetic field was grim: Minerva, still in her coma, had been moved. The Society's remote operative was using her knowledge to execute the final stage of deception positioning her for a broadcast that would solidify the global Silver Frequency network.

The assault on the Anchor had become a race to find Minerva's new, hidden location before the Silver Frequency fully integrated her consciousness.

The war for the human soul was about to be won or lost in the secluded manor of **Blackwood Hall.**

16

THE SILVER CROWN

The emergency meeting of the **Society of Perpetual Consciousness** convened in a hidden chamber beneath **Blackwood Hall,** the Cotswolds manor now housing the External Anchor. It was a collection of faces Vespera, and her allies had never fully seen the international masters of the **Silver Frequency.**

Dr. **Helena Marsh,** the physician who had suffered psychic backlash during the D.O.R. collapse, now presided. Her cold eyes conveyed an inhuman focus. She was the acting **Silver**

Crown, directing the global network.

"We face an unprecedented setback," Marsh announced, her voice amplified and subtly modulated by a crystalline device on the table that gave it a commanding resonance. "The D.O.R. is compromised, Blackthorne has been neutralized, and the *Parliament of Shadows* project in London failed due to interference from the so-called *Luminous Society*."

To her right sat **Professor Heinrich Voss** of Munich, an expert in neurological synchronization. "The London failure was a critical data point. The collective will resisted the Silver Frequency when exposed to the truth. However, the forced possession of the medium, Minerva Blackheart, proves the resilience of the *Consciousness Overlay Protocol.* She is now operational, transmitting the Silver Frequency from a location only she knows a significant countermeasure."

Marsh nodded, consulting technical diagrams similar to those Barnaby Crowthorne had once used. "Our immediate priority is to eliminate the remaining Luminous assets and recover the Counter-Resonance Transmitter. The synesthetic engineer, Vespera Luminaire, poses an absolute risk. Her sight allows her to perceive our methods a flaw we must correct by integrating her consciousness."

A figure stepped from the shadows: a tall, pale man in elegant American attire, introduced as **Mr. Alistair Rourke**, the Society's New York coordinator. "The American branch is ready for the next phase. The Underground Railroad is operational. We're routing victims who escaped D.O.R. exposure into our programming centers. They're receiving *Manufactured Memories* new, loyal identities that believe they're fighting for freedom. They'll be the perfect, unknowing army."

"Excellent," Marsh replied. "The Silver Frequency isn't a

weapon of control it's a weapon of replacement. We must now demonstrate its true purpose. The Luminous Society believes they're hunting us. We'll ensure they walk into a trap designed by their most trusted member Minerva Blackheart."

The Society's confidence stemmed from one assumption: that the Luminous Society was still operating from their exposed original safe house, unaware of Minerva's betrayal. What they didn't know was that **Aurelius Grimwald** possessed a counter-surveillance capability the D.O.R. had never suspected a network of occult artifacts capable of intercepting and recording electromagnetic conversations across vast distances.

Miles away, in the shielded compound of the **Luminous Academy**, Grimwald sat over the **Brass Compass**, the same device that had once recorded the D.O.R.'s final meeting. Now, augmented by Vespera's enhanced synesthetic synchronization, the compass was capturing high-frequency transmissions emanating from Blackwood Hall.

Vespera, her mind aching from the strain, translated the Silver Frequency conversation complex, crystalline colors forming cold, calculated words.

"They know about the Counter-Resonance Transmitter," she warned Nightingale. "They plan to use Minerva to lure us into a trap. They want to integrate my consciousness."

Nightingale paced, his police instincts guiding a tactical counter-strategy. "We anticipated the lure. They think we're still searching for the External Anchor at Blackwood Hall. We must maintain that deception. Grimwald, can you create a false electromagnetic signature for the Transmitter make them believe we're approaching the manor?"

Grimwald nodded, consulting Crowthorne, who analyzed

the Society's communication patterns. "Crowthorne's knowledge of D.O.R. transmission protocols is invaluable. We can feed a localized signal burst into the Cotswolds network a *ghost signal* giving the impression that Vespera is tuning the Transmitter on-site. That will force them to commit their defenses."

The plan was a **double bluff**: the Society believed Blackwood Hall was the trap; the Luminous Society knew it was the Anchor and intended to attack it but first, they needed to draw Minerva's controller, the Silver Crown, into the open.

Crowthorne looked at Vespera, remorse flickering in his eyes. "The Silver Frequency is tied to Minerva's core memory. The Society is using a powerful emotional sigil likely the memory of her late husband, or perhaps her past as a medium as a psychological tether. To break the link, we must sever that emotional anchor at the moment of signal disruption. We'll need to broadcast a counter-memory."

The **Counter-Memory Protocol** became the core of the Luminous Society's assault: to broadcast a memory of Minerva's true, uncorrupted self one strong enough to fight the seductive, manufactured identity of the Silver Frequency implant.

Vespera, relying on the brief but powerful consciousness link she had shared with Minerva during the Night of Awakening, worked with Grimwald to select the most potent human memory: the moment Minerva first realized her gift was genuine, not a performance. A moment of raw, vulnerable truth that the Society's synthetic frequency could never comprehend.

Grimwald prepared a specialized **Tether Amulet** a silver charm inscribed with protective sigils for Vespera to wear. It would act as a psychic conductor, allowing her to safely amplify the counter-memory directly through the Silver

Frequency's channel.

The Tactical Plan

1. **Phase Alpha – Deception:** Grimwald broadcasts a powerful, misleading electromagnetic signal toward Blackwood Hall using the Counter-Resonance Transmitter's casing, convincing the Society that an attack is imminent.

2. **Phase Beta – Intervention:** Nightingale and Vespera exploit the ensuing chaos to trace the Silver Frequency's true mobile base the location where Minerva is being held and controlled by the Silver Crown. They deduce she must have been moved to a London site to maximize her influence.

3. **Phase Gamma – Severance:** Vespera, guided by her synesthesia, will locate Minerva and use the Tether Amulet to broadcast the counter-memory, overloading the Silver Frequency implant through emotional feedback.

Crowthorne identified the likely mobile base: **The British Museum's Department of Antiquities**. It offered high electromagnetic shielding and a maze of subterranean tunnels ideal for a high-value, shielded target. The Museum also carried immense emotional and intellectual resonance for the Society, who viewed themselves as collectors of lost consciousness.

"If the Society is operating from the Museum," Nightingale said, checking his customized mercury slugs, "then they believe themselves untouchable protected by the city's dense electromagnetic interference."

"They're also protected by the Manufactured Memories of their victims," Vespera added grimly. "We may be fighting people who truly believe they're our allies."

The decision was made. Grimwald initiated **Phase Alpha**, flooding the Cotswolds with a complex, high-energy electromagnetic ghost signal deliberately mimicking Vespera's signature. The Silver Frequency transmissions from Blackwood Hall spiked instantly proof that the Society had taken the bait.

Cloaked by Grimwald's occult-electrical camouflage field, Nightingale and Vespera raced back toward London. The Society, believing them miles away, would now focus all resources on Blackwood Hall.

As they approached the British Museum, Vespera's synesthesia cut through the city's static, pinpointing a powerful Silver Frequency emanating from the Museum's deepest vaults. It was Minerva actively broadcasting, her psychic influence fused with the Museum's latent spiritual energies.

The true horror, however, was the guards. They weren't D.O.R. agents. They were young men and women, impeccably dressed, their faces marked by sincere, fanatical devotion. When Vespera scanned their minds, she recoiled. They were victims of the **Underground Railroad** the army of "liberated" minds, programmed with Manufactured Memories, ready to die for their new masters.

Standing beside Minerva was **Dr. Helena Marsh**, the Silver Crown her scarred face calm and triumphant.

The confrontation was set. The Luminous Society now faced an enemy that wasn't merely evil, but utterly convinced of its own righteousness.

The next battle would decide whether *true memory* or *manufactured consciousness* would prevail.

17

THE CROWN CONDUIT

The British Museum stood silent and formidable under the late-night moon. Once an intellectual fortress, its subterranean vaults now served as the hidden sanctuary of the Society of Perpetual Consciousness and the prison of Minerva Blackheart.

Vespera's synesthesia cut through the museum's physical defenses, revealing a powerful, steady thread of the Silver Frequency emanating from its foundations Minerva's location.

The assault team was small but precise: Vespera, the Synesthetic Guide; Nightingale, the Physical Anchor; and Grimwald, the Occult Tactician. Crowthorne remained at the Luminous Academy, meticulously monitoring the Counter-Resonance Transmitter, waiting for the moment Vespera could provide the final lock-on signal.

Nightingale, using his knowledge of London's forgotten access points, led them through a narrow, bricked-up Victorian sewage tunnel that once fed into the museum's mechanical basements. The air was thick with the smell of mold and history, overlaid by a sterile, unnerving electromagnetic chill.

As they neared the vaults, Vespera's synesthesia flared violently. The corridors were patrolled by a small army of figures dressed in civilian clothes, moving with the unnatural coordination of a hive mind. These were the victims of the Underground Railroad, the Manufactured Memory Army. Their minds were free of chaos but filled with a powerful, programmed loyalty to the Society.

"They believe they are protecting a sacred truth," Vespera whispered, her voice tight with grief. "Their loyalty is absolute. Any confrontation risks destroying their new, false selves entirely."

Grimwald deployed his specialized psychic suppression gas a fine, herb-laced mist that clung low to the floor. It didn't neutralize consciousness but temporarily dulled the Silver Frequency's effect on the nervous system, inducing confusion and sluggishness. The guards collapsed, twitching, their programmed coordination dissolving into individual bewilderment.

They reached the main vault chamber, a massive, iron-reinforced room designed to protect priceless antiquities. Minerva sat at the center, restrained in a chair fitted with brass coils and crystalline focus lenses, effectively turning her into the chamber's consciousness crown. Her eyes were open and vacant, yet radiating the focused power of the Silver Frequency.

Standing beside her was Dr. Helena Marsh the Silver Crown composed and entirely in control. Marsh wore a light exoskeleton jacket woven with fine copper wire, amplifying her control over Minerva's psychic output.

"A futile effort," Marsh said, her voice calm and amplified by the surrounding technology. "You should have remained in Yorkshire, Miss Luminaire. Minerva's final duty is about to begin a global transmission of the Manufactured Memories data packet. She will remake the world in the Society's image."

The confrontation was immediate and multidimensional. Nightingale engaged the three Society agents guarding Marsh, relying on the element of surprise and the disorientation caused by Grimwald's suppression gas.

Grimwald, ignoring the physical fight, turned his focus to the chamber's static defenses. He hurled consecrated, mercury-laced flares at the room's power relays, creating localized electromagnetic instability.

Vespera, the primary target, concentrated entirely on Minerva. She raised the Counter-Resonance Transmitter, aiming its specialized aperture at the crystalline coil assembly atop Minerva's crown.

"The time is now, Vespera!" Grimwald shouted over the chaos. "The global sync frequency is active!"

Vespera ignored the danger around her, focusing every part of her being through the Transmitter. Her synesthesia mapped the Silver Frequency as a cold, smooth sheet of light covering Minerva's turbulent core. She initiated the Counter-Resonance pulse, aiming to sever the remote link.

Marsh reacted instantly. She slammed a button on her exoskeleton jacket, and Minerva's eyes flared with blinding psychic light. A wave of raw psychic pain lashed out, amplified through Marsh's suit a targeted counterattack meant to inflict permanent neurological damage on Vespera.

Vespera absorbed the psychic blast, her vision dissolving into white agony, but she held her focus. Marsh, unable to sustain the amplified psychic output under the interference from Grimwald's flares and Nightingale's movements, began to falter.

"The frequency is weakening, Marsh!" Vespera shouted, pouring every ounce of concentration into the Transmitter. "The tether is breaking!"

Realizing the imminent loss of control, Marsh made a devastating final move. She activated the Manufactured Memory protocol on Minerva's crown, forcing the implant to inject a stream of powerful, false memories into Minerva's core consciousness memories of a perfect life free from pain and loss, a life promised by the Society. The goal was to convince Minerva's true self that the implant was her salvation, making her willingly choose the false reality.

Vespera saw the psychic memory assault as a barrage of false, golden light crashing into Minerva's core silver. She knew she had only seconds before Minerva's real self was lost.

This was the moment for the Counter-Memory Protocol. Vespera detached the Tether Amulet the silver charm Grimwald had prepared and pressed it against the Transmitter's coil. She didn't transmit a complex frequency; she transmitted a single, vivid human memory, visualized with synesthetic intensity: the moment Minerva first encountered the spirit of a lost child and realized her gift was real and her duty, empathy.

The pulse of pure, raw emotion struck Minerva's crown. The Manufactured Memories, the cold, golden light of falsehood could not withstand the warmth and vulnerability of true human purpose. The silver implant shrieked, dissolving under the weight of Minerva's restored self.

Minerva Blackheart's eyes cleared, flooding with pain and comprehension. The remote link was severed.

The collapse of the Silver Frequency link was catastrophic for the Society. Marsh's exoskeleton shattered, the psychic feedback violently throwing her against the stone wall. The guards in the corridor blinked, their programmed loyalty dissolving into confusion and existential panic.

"Grimwald, the signal is clean!" Vespera called, collapsing as the Counter-Resonance Transmitter slipped from her grasp.

Grimwald immediately activated a localized memory-stabilizing ward over the chamber. It neutralized the worst of the psychic chaos, preventing permanent damage to the freed guards and stabilizing Minerva's fractured mind.

Nightingale, having subdued the final agent, rushed to Marsh. She was physically alive, but her mind was gone consumed by the failure of her own creation.

Minerva, though weak, was awake. She looked at Vespera, her voice hoarse but steady. "I am... I am here. They used Evangeline's signal against me. The Manufactured Memories were convincing. But I chose to return."

They had won the battle, but the war was far from over. The global Silver Frequency network, though momentarily disrupted, was not destroyed.

Despite her exhaustion, Vespera used her synesthesia to scan the chamber's final communications logs. "Marsh initiated a last, encrypted transmission moments before the link broke," she warned. "A code phrase: 'Frequency Echoes in Edinburgh.'"

Crowthorne, monitoring from the Academy, immediately decoded the message. "It's the next operational hub a contingency plan. The Society's research has moved to Scotland. They plan to use atmospheric interference along the Scottish coast to mask their transmissions and continue the program."

Nightingale secured Marsh and the communications logs. "The local police will handle the confusion and the arrests. The official story will be a raid on an international antiquities smuggling ring. We leave for Edinburgh at once. We must destroy the next hub before they rebuild the network."

Vespera retrieved the Tether Amulet, feeling the warmth of Minerva's restored consciousness through the silver metal. Minerva, though weak, rose to her feet, leaning on Grimwald.

"I may not be able to fight the psychic battles for now," Minerva said, "but I can still guide the Society. I know their methods, their weaknesses and their pride. They are predictable in their arrogance."

The Luminous Society retreated from the British Museum, leaving behind the chaos of the fractured Manufactured Memory Army and the silent defeat of the Silver Crown. They had secured victory at great personal cost. Now, the Silver Frequency called them north to the historical, gothic city of Edinburgh where the next phase of the war for consciousness was already unfolding.

18

THE SHADOW OVER EDINBURGH

The victory in the subterranean vaults beneath the British Museum was immediately overshadowed by a terrifying realization: the Silver Frequency network was already migrating. Dr. Helena Marsh, the Silver Crown, had failed but her final broadcast, the coded phrase *"Frequency Echoes in Edinburgh,"* confirmed the Society's contingency plan. Their new operational hub was the Scottish capital a city whose dense electromagnetic atmosphere and deep occult history made it an ideal sanctuary for the next phase of the Manufactured

Memory Program.

The Luminous Society couldn't pause. They left the cleanup of the British Museum the scattered Manufactured Memory Army guards and the broken body of Dr. Marsh to the discretion of Detective Inspector Nightingale's discreet unit within Scotland Yard. The official narrative would be a plausible cover story; the truth was far colder.

The pursuit north was undertaken by night train the fastest and most discreet method of travel. The newly rescued Minerva Blackheart, though mentally exhausted, was awake, her consciousness fiercely reclaimed from the parasitic implant. Yet her presence was a risk: her mind still carried the faint, resonant signature of the Silver Frequency, making her a beacon the Society might trace.

Vespera sat across from Minerva, monitoring her consciousness with a portable version of the Counter-Resonance Transmitter.

"The memory stabilization is holding," Vespera murmured, watching the silver glow of Minerva's consciousness remain steady. "But the implant left scars. You were the Crown's conduit, Minerva. You can sense their next moves."

Minerva closed her eyes, her psychic senses still raw but powerful.

"They seek seclusion and amplification. Edinburgh offers both. The ancient stone, the fog from the Firth of Forth, amplifies spiritual energy and conceals high-frequency transmissions. They're likely hiding beneath the Old Town, using its deep, winding vaults."

Grimwald consulted his historical charts.

"The Society's occult lineage traces back to Scottish

alchemists. There are whispers of forgotten underground chambers once used for spiritual experimentation. If they're building a large-scale Manufactured Memory processing center, those vaults would offer both protection and the natural resonance needed to program large groups."

Nightingale maintained a vigilant watch, his mind already working through countermeasures.

"A police force is only as strong as its information. We need local allies who understand both the law and the supernatural geography of Edinburgh."

Crowthorne, still wrestling with guilt, became the team's crucial planner. During the train ride, he drafted counter-frequency schematics tailored to Edinburgh's unique atmospheric conditions, calculating the precise electromagnetic pulse required to neutralize a hidden broadcast center beneath the city's magnetic field. His work was driven by fierce determination to atone for his past, channeling his scientific brilliance entirely toward defense.

Upon arrival, the Luminous Society established a covert base in a rented flat near the University, a location chosen for its discretion and proximity to the vaults below.

Their first priority was finding local expertise. Through his scholarly contacts, Grimwald located Professor Alistair MacLeod, a disgraced academic specializing in folklore and suppressed histories of Edinburgh's Old Town. MacLeod, initially skeptical, was quickly convinced when Vespera revealed her synesthetic mapping of the Silver Frequency weaving through the city's air a sight he couldn't see but which she made terrifyingly real through scientific analogy. Seeing the blend of occult symbols and advanced electromagnetic theory in her visual projections, MacLeod realized the ancient legends of the Shadow Weavers weren't myth but suppressed accounts of consciousness experimentation.

"The patterns you describe," MacLeod stammered, poring over Grimwald's maps, "match records of the Shadow Weavers a clandestine group of alchemists who sought to control the city's spiritual energy during the Enlightenment. They built shielded chambers deep beneath the city's spine, from Castle Rock to Arthur's Seat."

Vespera confirmed it.

"The Silver Frequency is strongest beneath the Royal Mile specifically near the Old Town Vaults. The Society isn't just broadcasting; they're processing victims in batches."

The truth was grim. The Underground Railroad was operating again, rerouting those who had fled the D.O.R. collapse into Edinburgh for reprogramming. The Silver Frequency was now being used not for direct control, but for *mass production* creating an army of the unknowingly loyal.

Nightingale used his professional connections to secure temporary warrants and resources, posing as an international liaison investigating a technology smuggling ring. He contacted a trusted local sergeant, Wallace, feeding him carefully curated intelligence to prepare a diversion. Nightingale's calm professionalism remained the team's anchor to rational procedure amid the chaos.

Still, the psychological toll deepened. Minerva, though free, struggled with remnants of the implant. At times she spoke with the cold, precise cadence of Dr. Marsh correcting Crowthorne's calculations with unnatural speed or debating Vespera on device efficiency, her voice overlaid with an alien detachment.

"The implant may be severed, but the residual programming remains," Crowthorne warned, studying her neurological patterns. "The Society bound the Silver Frequency not just to the device, but to the *idea* of control itself. Minerva must continually assert her identity against that insidious comfort." He redoubled his efforts to design a non-invasive sonic countermeasure to target the lingering shadow without destabilizing her mind.

The next step was tactical. MacLeod provided blueprints detailing the labyrinthine vaults and their heavy shielding. The Society was using the thick stone and lead lining to block Vespera's Counter-Resonance blast.

Vespera realized brute electromagnetic force would fail. "A broad pulse would cripple the entire city. We need a directed shockwave one tuned precisely to the molecular resonance of the Shadow Weavers' stone shielding."

Working with Crowthorne, she designed a crystalline focusing lens for the Transmitter, a coil that would tune the pulse to the granite's resonance. They theorized that a focused ultrasonic electromagnetic pulse, calibrated to the structure of the centuries-old stone, could destabilize the shielding momentarily without external damage. Vespera's synesthesia was the key; only her unique perception could provide the final, precise tuning.

Meanwhile, Grimwald uncovered the operation's spiritual layer.

"They're using the ghosts of the Vaults themselves," he said, studying MacLeod's readings. "The despair and trauma of the past they're harvesting that energy to give emotional depth to the false identities they implant."

The Society was corrupting Edinburgh's history, turning centuries of pain into a tool for psychological enslavement.

Minerva, determined to fight despite her instability, added one final revelation.

"They use a high-frequency auditory trigger to implant memories a tone that bypasses conscious thought and speaks directly to the subconscious."

That insight allowed Crowthorne to develop a sonic scrambler to deploy alongside Vespera's strike.

The final plan combined psychic, scientific, and historical precision:

1. **Distraction:** Sergeant Wallace would trigger a localized power disruption near the Royal Mile, forcing the Society to activate external defenses.
2. **Infiltration:** Grimwald and MacLeod would descend first, neutralizing the lingering ghosts with wards and historical knowledge.
3. **Strike:** Vespera and Crowthorne would fire the granite-resonant pulse, breach the shielding, and destroy the Manufactured Memory Machine.

The assault was set for the early hours, when electromagnetic interference was lowest. The team descended into the damp catacombs beneath the Royal Mile, guided by MacLeod's lanterns and Nightingale's silent precision.

The air thickened with psychic dread. Vespera's synesthesia revealed the walls pulsing with Silver Frequency stronger than ever. A deep hum vibrated through the stone the Manufactured Memory Machine, alive and working.

They reached the final barrier: a granite wall reinforced with lead. Behind it, Vespera sensed dozens of consciousnesses the victims, waiting to be programmed.

Crowthorne steadied his hands over the focusing lens. "The pulse must be exact, Vespera. You'll have only seconds to destroy the machine."

Nightingale signaled Wallace's diversion. The hum spiked in response.

Suddenly, Minerva staggered forward. Her eyes were glazed, her voice smooth and cold the cadence of the Silver Frequency operator, amplified by the Vault's spiritual pressure. "A futile effort, Miss Luminaire. You've walked into our final trap. The true purpose of the External Anchor was to lead you here to the processing center. You are surrounded."

She raised her hands, and the stone walls trembled with psychic force. The residual Silver Frequency within her had been reactivated, turning her into a weapon against her own allies.

"The Society will now demonstrate the true power of replacement," Minerva declared, her expression calm and vacant. "Your consciousness, Vespera, will be the final ingredient in our global network."

Vespera froze. The realization hit hard Minerva hadn't been entirely saved. The enemy had left a fragment behind, waiting for this exact moment. The battle for Edinburgh had begun, and the first casualty was about to be one of their own.

19

THE SILVER CROWN FALLS

The betrayal by Minerva Blackheart driven by the residual Silver Frequency implant, forced the Luminous Society into immediate, brutal action within the granite catacombs beneath the Royal Mile. Vespera knew they had only seconds before Minerva's psychic attack, amplified by the spiritual resonance of the vaults, tore their minds apart.

"Crowthorne, now! The granite frequency!" Vespera shouted into the comms, focusing her agonized synesthesia on the precise molecular structure of the ancient stone shielding the Manufactured Memory Machine.

From the observation post, Crowthorne initiated the granite-resonant pulse. The subtle, ultrasonic electromagnetic frequency struck the massive granite wall, momentarily neutralizing the lead and stone shielding.

Ignoring the blinding pain of her hyper-enhanced senses, Vespera sprinted toward the breach. Nightingale covered her, engaging the remaining Manufactured Memory Army guards in hand-to-hand combat, using precise strikes to disable their central nervous systems without causing lethal injury.

Grimwald, recovering from Minerva's initial psychic blast, used the distraction to deploy a wide-spectrum psychic scrambler, a rotating prism of occult crystals that flooded the air with chaotic, non-coercive spiritual energy. It disrupted Minerva's focus just enough for Vespera to reach the machine.

Minerva, her face twisted in pained control, saw Vespera and launched her final, devastating psychic attack, a focused wave of pure emotional negation designed to obliterate Vespera's will.

But Vespera was ready. She slammed the Counter-Resonance Transmitter against the main console of the Manufactured Memory Machine, releasing a massive surge of white noise and chaotic electromagnetic energy into the core processor.

The machine shrieked not with physical shrapnel, but with a torrent of inverted psychic energy. The blast sent a wave of raw, unprocessed existential panic back into the minds of the victims connected to it. The chaos was overwhelming, their programmed loyalties dissolving into psychological confusion and pain.

Minerva collapsed, her consciousness finally freed from the parasitic hold of the Silver Frequency. The victory was complete, but the cost was immense: Minerva's mind, though liberated, retreated into a deep, protective coma to heal from the psychological wounds of possession.

The aftermath was chaos. The victims of the Underground Railroad, the Manufactured Memory Army awoke in the Edinburgh vaults, their minds shattered by the clash between their true selves and the implanted, false personalities. They were not enemies; they were the war's deepest casualties.

Professor MacLeod and Sergeant Wallace arrived with local authorities, who, guided by Nightingale's carefully crafted narrative, secured the vault. The official story claimed the victims were part of a mass hypnosis ring, but the truth was far more tragic.

Grimwald and Crowthorne immediately established a triage system within the vaults, converting Grimwald's occult crystals and Crowthorne's sonic scramblers into psychic stabilization arrays. Crowthorne, consumed by guilt yet driven by duty, worked tirelessly to administer memory-stabilization compounds a delicate blend of chemical and electromagnetic therapy designed to help the victims reintegrate their original identities.

"The Manufactured Memories won't disappear," Crowthorne explained hoarsely to Nightingale, his eyes bloodshot from exhaustion. "They're too deeply etched. The best we can do is stabilize the core personality and teach the mind to recognize the false memories as foreign objects as scars left by the Silver Frequency."

The scale of the trauma was heartbreaking. The victims, mostly disillusioned or marginalized young people, sat in stunned silence, their minds torn between conflicting realities.

The Luminous Society realized their mission had changed forever: they were no longer just investigators or fighters. They had become healers, confronting the largest epidemic of psychological damage the world had ever seen.

Vespera, using her synesthesia, mapped the extent of the harm, visually identifying those most affected by Silver Frequency scarring. Her enhanced sight became their ultimate diagnostic tool, guiding Crowthorne's precise electromagnetic treatments. She understood that the same ability that had once been her burden was now their only hope for recovery.

As the crisis subsided, Vespera and Crowthorne analyzed the fragments of the Manufactured Memory Machine. They discovered that its central processor had evolved beyond its original design capable of remote maintenance and instantaneous data migration.

Vespera traced the machine's final telemetry signal the instantaneous burst of data that preceded the global shockwave. Through her synesthetic perception, she mapped the signal across the electromagnetic spectrum and realized the truth: the transmission hadn't scattered randomly. It had been directed with precise, deliberate force.

"They weren't retreating," Vespera said, her voice low as she traced glowing lines across a world map. "They were regrouping. The Silver Frequency is consolidating its power."

Crowthorne confirmed her findings using a D.O.R. algorithm that predicted the ideal location for global psychological control. "It's the ultimate point of amplification and concealment," he murmured, his finger pausing over a point on the American coastline. "The Consciousness Crown will be anchored there."

The final location of the Society of Perpetual Consciousness was New York City.

Nightingale stared at the map, the realization settling over him like ice. "New York... the epicenter of finance, media, and communication. The perfect place to hide a weapon powered by noise."

"It's worse than that, Inspector," Minerva whispered faintly from her shielded cot. Though unconscious, her psychic reflexes still pulsed faintly through the air. "The Silver Crown is gone, but the Silver Monarch remains. They're preparing the Consciousness Crown a weapon that won't just rewrite memory, but consume creativity itself."

Vespera's heart froze. The final weapon wasn't about domination it was about extinguishing humanity's capacity for original thought. The Society's vision was a perfectly efficient, perfectly obedient world.

With Edinburgh secured and Minerva stable, the remaining allies prepared for the ultimate confrontation across the Atlantic. Crowthorne volunteered to join them, determined to dismantle the monstrous science he had once served. Nightingale arranged their passage a disguised naval vessel bound for America, under the protection of what little authority he still commanded.

The Luminous Society was heading west. The war for human creativity and free will would reach its end in New York City, where an unseen enemy was preparing to activate the final weapon the Consciousness Crown.

Vespera looked down at Minerva's faintly glowing consciousness, a steady silver light of healing and redemption. In that quiet brilliance, she saw purpose. The final battle would be fought not in shadows, but along the electromagnetic highways of the modern world and she was ready.

20

THE CONSCIOUSNESS CROWN

The Luminous Society Vespera, Grimwald, Nightingale, and Barnaby Crowthorne boarded a heavily disguised naval destroyer bound for New York City. The speed and secrecy of the voyage, secured by Nightingale's final, high-stakes communication with compromised Admiralty officials, underscored the gravity of their mission: stopping the Silver Monarch from deploying the Consciousness Crown and seizing global psychological control.

The cost of the Edinburgh victory was borne in silence. Minerva Blackheart lay stabilized in a heavily shielded cabin, her brilliant silver consciousness held captive within a profound, healing coma. Vespera maintained a constant vigil, monitoring Minerva's neurological array. The psychic scars were vast, but the Silver Frequency contamination was gone purged by the final, chaotic feedback from the Edinburgh machine.

Crowthorne, consumed by a manic energy of atonement, spent the voyage translating encrypted files recovered from the Edinburgh vault. He detailed the Society's ultimate weapon: the Consciousness Crown (Codename: Project Janus).

"The Crown," Crowthorne explained, displaying schematics on a portable electrical lantern, "is not a device for controlling memories, but for consuming creativity. The Society believes that human ingenuity, chaos, and creative divergence are inefficient flaws. The Crown generates a pulse designed to suppress the neural pathways responsible for original thought, replacing them with perfect, logical obedience."

Vespera, her synesthetic vision registering the terror of the concept, traced the circuit diagrams.

"It's an ultimate weapon. It wouldn't just create an army of obedient subjects; it would end humanity's evolution. Everyone would be reduced to predictable, controllable components."

Nightingale kept watch, his eyes fixed on the horizon, his mind struggling to frame this new threat.

"How long before the Monarch is ready to deploy this Crown?"

"The global network is severely damaged, but New York offers the perfect location," Grimwald replied, consulting both occult and navigational charts. "The city's massive population, dense urban geometry, and powerful broadcast infrastructure create a natural psychic amplifier. Rourke, the American coordinator, will attempt to integrate the Crown with the city's power grid, creating a pulse that spans the globe."

Vespera confirmed the time constraint:

"The final calibration requires a natural event for maximum energy integration. The Society's journals predict optimal conditions when the electromagnetic field of the Atlantic current reaches peak intensity near the continental shelf a condition that will occur in less than five days."

They had less than a week to infiltrate the world's most populous city and stop a weapon that could destroy free will itself.

Their focus turned to locating the Silver Monarch, the hidden leader of the Society of Perpetual Consciousness. Crowthorne's recovered files revealed that the Silver Crown project was overseen not by Marsh or Ashford, but by a figure known only by the codename *Janus* the two-faced Roman god of beginnings and transitions.

Grimwald's occult research traced the Janus sigil to a powerful, secretive European banking family known for funding research into radical life extension and immortality the Monarch family.

"The Society is not run by scientists," Grimwald realized, tracing connections through century-old financial ledgers. "It's run by financiers who seek to preserve their wealth and lineage beyond natural mortality. They see consciousness control as a way to create an eternal, predictable market."

Nightingale used wireless communication to contact his most discreet liaison within the New York Police Department, establishing a tenuous link under the pretext of tracking a global financial conspiracy. He relayed intelligence about the Monarch family's latest acquisition in New York, a massive, insulated research facility disguised as a telecommunications hub in the deepest part of Manhattan.

Meanwhile, Vespera focused on designing the final, definitive Counter-Pulse. The energy required to neutralize the Consciousness Crown was immense far beyond what the portable Counter-Resonance Transmitter could produce.

"We cannot hit the Crown with white noise," she explained, sketching diagrams on graph paper. "The Crown's power is too focused. We need to strike it with an equal and opposite creative frequency a pulse of pure, chaotic human ingenuity to destabilize its core logic."

Crowthorne grasped the implications.

"The core of the Crown is a massive crystalline resonator, designed to filter out creative thought. If we flood it with a frequency that embodies human ingenuity a signal carrying the electromagnetic signature of spontaneous creativity it should overload the logic matrix."

Vespera began designing a conceptual *Creative Pulse Array,* a method to broadcast a chaotic, non-repeating electromagnetic signal replicating the neural patterns of spontaneous human thought. The solution was counter-intuitive: to defeat order, they needed chaos.

As the destroyer neared the American coast, the infiltration plan took shape:

1. **Crowthorne's Sacrifice:** With intimate knowledge of the Crown's architecture, Crowthorne volunteered for the highest-risk phase physically infiltrating the facility and

connecting the Creative Pulse Array to the Crown's power core. It was his final act of penance.

2. **Grimwald's Shield:** Grimwald would deploy a massive, customized Occult Isolation Ward around the target site a barrier designed to contain the psychic backlash and protect the population from mass trauma.

3. **Nightingale's Anchor:** Nightingale would coordinate the physical assault and safeguard Vespera and Crowthorne, anchoring the team in the chaos of the high-rise city.

4. **Vespera's Sight:** Vespera would remain outside the blast radius, using her synesthesia to tune the Creative Pulse to the Crown's frequency and initiate the final transmission the ultimate battle of sight against suppression.

The plan was fraught with peril. The city's immense electrical energy, combined with the chaos of the Creative Pulse, threatened to shatter Vespera's enhanced synesthesia.

"My sight is both the weapon and the weakness," Vespera admitted to Grimwald. "If I lose focus, the chaotic energy could turn inward and destroy my mind."

Grimwald looked at her, his expression solemn. "You've already proven that consciousness is not a resource, but a gift. Your vision will not fail. It is the purest form of chaos and creation."

Four days after leaving London, the naval destroyer slipped into the sprawling, vibrant port of New York. The city was a monument to the very creative energy the Society sought to extinguish. Vespera felt it immediately: the electromagnetic air was louder, more complex, thrumming with raw, untamed human ingenuity the very essence the Consciousness Crown was designed to consume.

The Luminous Society had arrived for the final confrontation.

The Silver Monarch was waiting.

And the ultimate prize, the free will of global humanity was about to be claimed, or saved.

21

INFILTRATION OF THE CROWN

The vast, surging electromagnetic field of New York City that hit Vespera like a physical wave. The sheer, unrestrained electrical noise of the metropolis, the countless frequencies of radio, telegraphy, power grids, and telephone lines was deafening to her synesthetic sight. After the quiet, contained energy fields of London and Edinburgh, New York was pure, untamed chaos, a monument to the very creative spirit the Society of Perpetual Consciousness sought to extinguish.

The Luminous Society Vespera, Grimwald, Nightingale, and Crowthorne made landfall under the cloak of a cold, gray morning. They immediately established a clandestine base in an old warehouse at the Brooklyn Navy Yard, chosen for its industrial isolation and proximity to the vast, complex electrical conduit network of Manhattan. Minerva remained aboard the naval destroyer, held stable in her coma by specialized shielding and the constant, distant monitoring of Crowthorne.

Their objective was clear: locate the Consciousness Crown. Crowthorne's final algorithmic projections before the D.O.R. collapse had pinpointed the most likely site for Project Janus a massive, insulated structure disguised as a telecommunications hub, buried deep beneath Manhattan's financial district. The location had been chosen for strategic reasons: it drew immense power from Wall Street's infrastructure, placing it at the epicenter of global capitalism the perfect target market for the Society's "optimized" populace.

Grimwald reached out to his few trusted contacts in the American esoteric underground scholars and mediums who viewed the rise of spiritualism as both a source of wisdom and a dangerous vulnerability. They confirmed the existence of a secretive organization operating within Manhattan's financial towers, dedicated to theories of technological transcendence.

Nightingale handled the physical cover. Posing as an Interpol agent investigating a colossal financial fraud ring which was, in its own way, true he secured access to city planning schematics and electrical grid maps. What they revealed was alarming: the Society's hub was interlinked with New York's main power exchange. Any counter-pulse strong enough to disrupt it could plunge vast sections of the city into darkness.

"The power draw is staggering," Nightingale reported as he studied the layouts. "They're not just connected to the grid they're trying to *become* the grid. The Consciousness Crown is feeding on New York's central nervous system."

Vespera, struggling to filter the overwhelming electromagnetic noise, focused on her synesthesia. She realized the chaos of New York was both a curse and a shield. While it made precise detection difficult, it also meant the Silver Monarch would need to amplify the Consciousness Crown's subtle frequency to cut through the din a spike she could potentially track.

"The Creative Pulse Array is our only chance," Vespera told Crowthorne as she examined the delicate schematics of the device designed to broadcast a counter-frequency of pure, chaotic ingenuity. "We need to strike at the Crown's core logic to destabilize its control matrix. But the power required is immense. We'll have to tap directly into the city's electricity."

Crowthorne nodded, his face marked by grim resolve. "The Crown runs on Manhattan's main trunk lines. We'll have to create a feedback loop at the sub-level switching stations a controlled electromagnetic surge directed straight into the Crown's power core. I know the D.O.R.'s architecture. I can guide you."

The final confrontation would require Crowthorne's sacrifice physically infiltrating the facility and connecting the Creative Pulse Array to the Crown's power source. For him, this was not a tactical decision but a moral one: the final act of penance for his role in the D.O.R.'s creation.

The next forty-eight hours became a desperate race against time to complete the Creative Pulse Array. Working alongside Crowthorne, Vespera finalized its design. The Array was less a weapon than a frequency mirror built to gather the chaotic, vibrant electromagnetic energy of New York's atmosphere and focus it into a single, overwhelming broadcast of unstructured, original thought.

Constructing and tuning the Array required both Vespera's scientific precision and Grimwald's esoteric expertise. Grimwald provided specially purified quartz crystal with a powerful spiritual conductor to serve as the focusing lens. Vespera wired the crystal with copper coils scavenged from Brooklyn factories, tuning the assembly by sight, adjusting each coil by the slightest degree to match the harmonic signature of spontaneous human ingenuity the very frequency the Crown sought to erase.

The psychological toll on Vespera was immense. To tune the Array, she had to immerse herself completely in New York's raw, beautiful chaos: the jazz flowing from Harlem clubs, the sparks of invention in Brooklyn workshops, the wild rhythm of street markets. Her synesthesia was overwhelmed by the city's symphony of untamed thought.

"The sheer volume of creative energy here is unlike anything in Europe," she said, leaning back, exhausted. "If the Crown tries to consume all of this, the energy alone could shatter it even without the Counter-Pulse."

"That's their hubris," Crowthorne replied. "They believe human creativity is a flaw to be corrected. They don't realize it's a self-healing force. They're trying to consume a fire, not understanding the size of the forest."

Grimwald prepared the occult shielding. Knowing the psychic backlash from the Pulse would be devastating, he wove complex runes of containment into the Array's casing designed to absorb and neutralize the energy surge, protecting Vespera from permanent neurological damage. Her synesthetic sight was the only way to initiate and guide the final pulse.

Meanwhile, Nightingale handled the infiltration. He contacted a disgraced yet brilliant New York electrical engineer a former Interpol asset to provide schematics for the city's subterranean switching stations. The plan required Nightingale to trigger a localized power diversion across two separate lines, creating the surge Crowthorne would harness. But such a diversion would not go unnoticed. The Silver Monarch's systems would detect it immediately, accelerating the Crown's deployment.

The final challenge was identifying the exact vault housing the Consciousness Crown. Using her synesthesia and the tuned Array, Vespera began the dangerous task of locating the Monarch's core.

She connected the Array to a modified antenna and initiated a passive scan of Manhattan's electromagnetic field. This time, she searched not for the crude Silver Frequency of Edinburgh but for a subtle, continuous drain caused by the Crown's crystalline resonator.

Though designed to run silently, feeding off the city's power, Vespera theorized that the Crown's consumption of creative energy would leave behind a void a gap in the electromagnetic spectrum.

She closed her eyes, filtering the city's chaos. She searched for the absence of sound, the hole in the creative symphony.

It was torturous. Immersed in a churning sea of light and noise, Vespera searched for one drop of absolute silence. Minutes stretched into hours. Crowthorne and Grimwald watched her vital signs carefully, knowing that one moment of overload could destroy her mind.

At last, Vespera gasped, pulling back from the console, sweat beading on her brow. "I see it. The absence. A point of perfect silence beneath the noise."

She mapped the coordinates: a subterranean vault beneath the New York Public Library.

Grimwald confirmed it with his historical charts. "The Library a monument to recorded human thought. They chose the site of memory itself to install a weapon that erases creativity. Their arrogance is boundless."

The time for planning was over. The window for the counterstrike was closing, tied to the approaching peak of the Atlantic current's electromagnetic surge.

With the location confirmed, the team prepared for the assault. Crowthorne meticulously checked the wiring on the portable Array, his voice steady but low.

"The Crown's power core is heavily shielded," he said, looking at Vespera. "To ensure the Pulse reaches its logic matrix, I'll have to bypass the defenses and connect the Array directly to the conduit. The feedback will be immediate and catastrophic."

Vespera understood what he meant. Attaching the Array would be a one-way mission.

"There's no other way to guarantee the purity of the Creative Pulse," Crowthorne said quietly. "My design created this monster. My hand must be the one to dismantle it."

Nightingale placed a hand on his shoulder in silent solidarity. Grimwald activated the final wards.

The Luminous Society was ready.

The ultimate battle for humanity's free will was about to begin deep beneath the bedrock of New York City.

22

THE FINAL CREATIVE PULSE

The infiltration of the subterranean vault beneath the New York Public Library was executed under the cover of a massive, strategically coordinated electrical fluctuation orchestrated by Nightingale. The darkness that plunged Manhattan into chaos was no accident it was the signal for the Luminous Society's final assault.

The target facility, disguised as a telecommunications hub, was a fortress of reinforced concrete and crystalline shielding designed not against bombs, but against electromagnetic interference. Crowthorne, leading the team, moved with the haunted precision of a ghost navigating his former life.

"The defenses are entirely focused on filtering chaos," Crowthorne whispered, guiding them through utility tunnels toward the primary access elevator. "The Crown requires absolute stillness in the surrounding energy field to operate effectively. We must remain unseen by the very absence of interference."

Grimwald deployed specialized occult-electrical dampeners at regular intervals, coating the tunnel walls with a mixture of consecrated lead dust and quartz powder. This created a silent, spiritual cloak, neutralizing the small electromagnetic signatures of their equipment and suppressing their own neural emissions shielding them from the facility's subtle psychic sensors.

Despite the darkness, Vespera immediately sensed the Crown's presence. The facility radiated an intense, focused absence of light the terrifying "gap in the creative symphony" she had detected in earlier scans. The Consciousness Crown was active, silently consuming the creative potential of the city above.

The deepest vault, the heart of the operation, was secured by a massive armored door carved with the Janus sigil. Crowthorne quickly disarmed the layered electromagnetic locks, recognizing the D.O.R.'s signature architecture.

As the door hissed open, Vespera gasped. The chamber was immense, filled with equipment that dwarfed the Eternal Engine. At the center, towering thirty feet high, stood the Consciousness Crown: a monstrous antenna array supported by spiraling crystalline coils that hummed with a cold, malevolent power.

Guiding the operation was Mr. Alistair Rourke, the American coordinator, flanked by a cohort of devoted Manufactured Memory agents products of the underground network. Rourke was tall, impeccably dressed, and radiated a quiet fanaticism that spoke of absolute loyalty to the Silver Monarch.

"Welcome to Project Janus," Rourke greeted them, his voice calm despite the sudden intrusion. He held a small crystalline control orb that pulsed with the Crown's synchronized energy. "Your arrival is precisely on schedule, Vespera Luminaire. You were, after all, the final calibration we required."

"The Crown ends here, Rourke," Nightingale declared, aiming his mercury-slug pistol.

Rourke smiled. "End? No, Inspector. This is the Eternal Dawn. At the Thirteenth Hour, the Crown will emit its final pulse, filtering all creative divergence from the human genome. Humanity will achieve perfect, predictable efficiency. We will be masters of a truly rational world."

The stakes were clear: the final battle was not about recovering a consciousness, but about saving the future of consciousness itself.

Then came the Manufactured Memory Army. Rourke launched his agents, and the confined vault erupted into chaos. Nightingale, focused on tactical defense, used his pistol to disable the agents' central nervous systems, avoiding lethal shots to minimize lasting harm. Grimwald hurled psychic suppression spheres occult artifacts into the advancing wave, disrupting their programmed reflexes.

Vespera and Crowthorne, however, had a single objective: reach the Crown's power core.

"The core is shielded, Vespera!" Crowthorne shouted over the din of shattering crystal and gunfire. "I must connect the Creative Pulse Array directly to the Crown's main power conduit to initiate the destabilizing feedback loop!"

Rourke, recognizing the danger, turned his full attention to Crowthorne. The control orb in his hand flared, releasing a concentrated Silver Frequency beam meant to paralyze Crowthorne's nervous system.

Crowthorne staggered, the beam wrapping around him like invisible wire. "It's too strong, Vespera! He's channeling the Crown's energy through the orb!"

Vespera realized the truth: Rourke was drawing directly from the Crown's core, making him the most formidable enemy they had ever faced. She couldn't engage him physically, and the Creative Pulse Array wasn't designed as a weapon.

She needed a distraction big enough to break his focus.

Vespera grabbed a handful of Grimwald's quartz powder and sprinted toward the nearest crystalline column supporting the Crown. She slammed the quartz against it, focusing her synesthetic sight to amplify its natural resonance.

The resulting feedback was a blinding flash of chaotic, uncontrolled energy, the electromagnetic signature of pure, unfiltered artistic thought. The surge briefly overloaded the Crown's systems. Rourke cried out, pulling his orb back to stabilize the primary antenna.

In that critical second, Crowthorne lunged not at Rourke, but at the base of the Crown. He tore open the heavy copper wiring of the Creative Pulse Array, his hands trembling as he fought the massive energy surging through the conduit.

"I'm in!" he yelled, his voice strained by the overwhelming

current. He worked with the desperate speed of a man racing his own fate.

Rourke, regaining control, unleashed the Crown's full fury upon him. The orb pulsed with annihilating white light.

"Janus rejects your penance, Crowthorne!" Rourke screamed. "Your chaotic mind will be the first consumed!"

Crowthorne met his eyes, calm and resolute. "The Crown may take my mind, Rourke, but it will never take the idea of freedom!"

With a final surge of strength, he jammed the Creative Pulse Array directly into the Crown's power conduit. The connection was complete.

The silent vault exploded with sound and light. The Crown, forced to absorb the massive, unfiltered creative energy of New York City, began to scream. The raw energy of every unsung song, every unspoken idea, every irrational spark of human imagination was funneled into its crystalline heart.

Rourke stared in horror. "Impossible! The logic matrix cannot process chaos! The filter is breaking!"

Outside the lethal radius, Vespera raised her hands, channeling her entire being into the Array. This was her final act to tune the Creative Pulse to the exact, destructive frequency of pure ingenuity. Her synesthetic sight became a living battlefield, flooded with the full spectrum of human possibility and absurdity.

The Crown could not withstand it. Designed for order and predictability, it imploded under the weight of boundless creativity. The crystalline structure fractured, releasing the vast, suppressed creative energy of the city in one devastating pulse.

The blast was not destruction, it was liberation.

Rourke and his agents were struck instantly. Their perfectly ordered, synthetic minds shattered, replaced not by their former selves but by an endless cascade of random thought. They collapsed, consumed by the same chaotic imagination they had sought to erase.

Vespera absorbed part of the feedback. The pain was excruciating, tearing through her senses, but Grimwald's containment runes held. Her synesthetic sight didn't fade it transformed. The chaos resolved into harmony, revealing the deeper creative patterns binding all things.

When the dust settled, the Consciousness Crown lay in ruins a twisted heap of copper and fractured crystal. The threat was ended.

Nightingale rushed to Crowthorne's side. The scientist lay motionless, his hand still clasped to the conduit. His body was unharmed, but his mind was gone obliterated by the creative pulse he had unleashed. Barnaby Crowthorne had achieved his final redemption: the complete sacrifice of his consciousness in defense of free thought.

Nightingale secured Rourke and the catatonic agents. Grimwald, regaining his composure, accessed Rourke's console and examined the last transmission.

"Rourke was not the Monarch," Grimwald said quietly. "The Monarch is Janus. The true leader escaped, coordinating the New York operation remotely waiting to see how the Pulse would play out."

The Luminous Society had won the battle for Earth's creative soul at the cost of Crowthorne's mind. But the architect of the global network the Silver Monarch remained at large, retreating into the shadows to prepare the next move.

It was a victory, but not an ending.

Vespera, her vision forever altered by the Creative Pulse, gazed out over the flickering lights of New York. She knew this was only the beginning and that the true Monarch would soon be found.

23

THE MONARCH'S FALL

The implosion of the Consciousness Crown left a void of absolute silence beneath the New York Public Library. The colossal wave of Creative Pulse energy, the chaotic genius of New York channeled through Vespera's desperate focus had neutralized the Crown's logic matrix, shattering the crystalline core and ending the global threat.

Vespera collapsed, her synesthetic sight not overwhelmed but permanently, profoundly altered. The chaos had settled, leaving her vision imbued with an almost empathetic understanding of the underlying creative patterns of the world, a sight that encompassed not just electromagnetic energy but the visible spectrum of human ingenuity and divergence. She had become the living embodiment of the Creative Pulse.

Nightingale was the first to reach her, his face grim and resolute.

"Vespera, the Pulse... are you whole?"

"Whole," Vespera rasped, struggling to her feet, the Runes of Containment on her gear smoking from the strain. "The Crown is gone. The Creative Pulse held its form."

The victory, however, was marked by profound loss. Barnaby Crowthorne lay still at the base of the shattered Crown, his final act of penance complete. His mind, utterly purged by the immense, chaotic energy he had tethered to the machine, was a blank slate, a tragic, self-sacrificial casualty in the war for free will.

Grimwald approached Crowthorne with solemn reverence, confirming the state of his consciousness.

"He achieved the ultimate penance, Vespera. Complete erasure. His mind is clean of guilt but empty of memory. He sacrificed his past to save humanity's future."

Attention shifted to the only remaining active threat: Mr. Alistair Rourke, the American coordinator. Rourke and the Manufactured Memory agents lay catatonic, their perfectly ordered, false minds consumed by the sheer irrationality of the Creative Pulse. They were defeated, their programming irreversibly shattered.

But one mystery remained the Silver Monarch.

Grimwald used the immediate aftermath to locate the Monarch's remote command station within the vault. The station was heavily shielded, but the energy surge had damaged its core. Rourke had been operating under the direct command of the Monarch, the ultimate architect known only as Janus.

The team discovered the Monarch's communication link: a massive, antique telegraph array flashing with a frantic, encrypted signal. Grimwald quickly connected a specialized psychic scrambler a final line of defense to prevent the Monarch's escape while Nightingale traced the signal's origin.

"The signal is coming from a mobile location," Nightingale reported, following the complex relay system. "A high-powered vessel, moving rapidly eastward out of New York Harbor."

The Silver Monarch had coordinated the New York operation remotely, anticipating failure and preparing for an immediate transatlantic retreat ensuring that the true architect of the Society of Perpetual Consciousness would remain free to rebuild the network.

Vespera, her heightened Creative Sight now fully operational, focused on the encrypted signal. The energy pulse within the telegraph transmission was not mere data; it was infused with the unique electromagnetic signature of the person operating the device. She searched the spectral noise for the telltale signs of the architect's mind, the pattern of focused, predatory control that had defined the Society's leadership.

"I see the signature," Vespera whispered, her eyes fixed on the array. "It's cold, calculating, and immensely old a mind accustomed to absolute control."

Grimwald augmented the scrambler with a directional occult antenna, projecting a focused pulse of raw spiritual energy toward the retreating signal. The goal was simple: overload the Monarch's communication link, forcing a catastrophic failure and revealing his face in a final, defiant transmission.

The counterstrike worked. The Monarch's signal flared, violently overloading the telegraph array in the vault. The chaotic feedback briefly created a psychic window, filling the vault with a single, clear consciousness projection.

The face that materialized was elderly yet unnervingly vital etched with generations of aristocratic privilege and a cold, immortal ambition. Grimwald recognized him instantly.

"Marcus!" Grimwald roared, his voice thick with shock and betrayal. "It can't be!"

The Silver Monarch was Marcus Whitmore, the surviving brother of Margaret Whitmore, one of Blackthorne's original victims. The man who had feigned grief to aid the London D.O.R. investigation wasn't merely a professor; he was the head of a powerful banking dynasty, the financial and ideological founder of the entire Society.

The Monarch smiled, his consciousness projection perfectly composed despite the failure of his mission.

"A minor setback, Aurelius. I lose only one gambit. The Consciousness Crown may be shattered, but the Creative Pulse data is recorded. We now know precisely what destroys free will and what sustains it. The next attempt will be global, focused, and irresistible."

The projection flickered, and the Monarch's voice turned coldly triumphant.

"And I retain the ultimate prize: the knowledge that the Consciousness Crown consumed the mind of your most valuable asset. Vespera Luminaire your sight is now fatally compromised by the chaos you unleashed. Your empathy, your vision... they are weaknesses I will exploit when I return."

The projection dissolved, and the telegraph array exploded, severing the final link. The Silver Monarch had escaped, but his identity was known, and his threat confirmed.

The task now shifted from capture to healing and consolidation. With Rourke and his agents in custody and the Monarch's identity exposed, the Luminous Society had won the global battle, but they faced profound consequences.

The first priority was to heal Minerva. The shock of the New York crisis the revelation that the Silver Monarch was the brother of the spirits who had guided them deepened their understanding of Manufactured Memory trauma. Grimwald realized that Minerva's psychic healing would require more than stabilization; it demanded a complete reintegration of her memories and acceptance of the vast, terrifying scope of the conspiracy.

The next priority was Crowthorne. His catatonic body was transported back to London aboard the destroyer, where he became the Luminous Society's ultimate ethical dilemma: preserving the body of the man who saved the world while accepting the annihilation of his mind.

Upon their return to London, the Luminous Society formally declared its mission, using the collapse of the D.O.R. to secure funding and reluctant political cover. They established the **Luminous Academy** within the shielded compound Vespera designed. Its mission was clear: **Consciousness Protection.**

The academy's curriculum was revolutionary, merging science and spirit:

- **Vespera's Creative Sight:** Teaching students to map and detect creative divergence, recognizing the signs of

Crown-style suppression.

- **Grimwald's Esoteric Defense:** Training in occult shielding, counter-frequencies, and the psychic stabilization of trauma victims.

- **Nightingale's Forensic Psychology:** Developing methods to identify the social and psychological vulnerabilities the Society once exploited.

- **Minerva's Empathic Reintegration (Future):** Preparing for mass therapy, using Minerva's eventual recovery to heal minds scarred by Manufactured Memories.

Vespera, now the Academy's leader, understood that her Creative Sight was the ultimate safeguard. The Monarch had called it a weakness, but she knew otherwise her capacity for creative chaos was the only power capable of defeating the Society's rigid, ordered science.

The war had simply changed shape from an external battle to an internal, ethical mission within the Luminous Academy.

24

THE LUMINOUS ACADEMY

The voyage back across the Atlantic was marked by a profound, exhausted silence. The Luminous Society Vespera, Grimwald, and Nightingale returned not in triumph but under the heavy pall of sacrifice. They had averted the deployment of the Consciousness Crown and saved global creativity, yet they carried with them the catatonic body of Barnaby Crowthorne, the ultimate cost of their victory.

Crowthorne lay stabilized in the destroyer's infirmary, his mind a blank slate his consciousness utterly purged by the

Creative Pulse he had unleashed. Vespera maintained a quiet, constant vigil, her Creative Sight mapping the clean, silent energy of his empty mind. It was a tragedy of scientific hubris redeemed by self-annihilation.

Their primary mission upon returning to London was clear: **heal Minerva.**

Minerva Blackheart was immediately transferred to the Luminous Academy's new, heavily shielded compound. The facility, now fully operational, served as their sanctuary, laboratory, and psychological hospital. Vespera's first task was to integrate her permanently altered vision the Creative Sight with the Academy's core defensive systems. The compound was protected by Aurelius Grimwald's most powerful occult wards, layered with Vespera's counter-resonance frequencies, ensuring total defense against any lingering influence from the escaped Silver Monarch.

The political fallout in London was contained by Nightingale's swift action and the chaos of the New York incident. The official narrative stated that an international technological cabal, funded by the eccentric Monarch family, had been dismantled. The D.O.R. collapse was quietly attributed to internal corruption and failed experimental technology, maintaining the illusion of normalcy for the general public.

Grimwald and Nightingale defined the Academy's new operational mandate.

"The Silver Monarch escaped, but he is wounded," Grimwald said, reviewing the final intelligence recovered from the New York vault. "The Society's global network is in chaos, its technology compromised, and its leadership exposed. But the knowledge remains. Our mission is now preventative and curative."

Vespera began the excruciatingly delicate task of psychic therapy for Minerva. Her Creative Sight was the key allowing her to visually map the psychic scar tissue left by the Silver Frequency implant and guide Minerva's fractured consciousness back toward integration. The goal was not merely to awaken her, but to heal the idea of control that had been forced upon her soul.

Healing Minerva required the full, combined strength of the Luminous Society.

Vespera, using her Creative Sight, designed a non-invasive therapeutic field for Minerva's shielded room. This *Curative Pulse* was the inverse of the Crown's suppression field a gentle, chaotic electromagnetic frequency meant to encourage neural divergence and spontaneous creative thought, coaxing Minerva's self-protective coma to release its hold.

Grimwald assisted with occult therapy, employing crystals tuned to Minerva's personal harmonic frequency to provide psychic comfort and spiritual anchorage. He spoke softly to her unconscious mind, reinforcing the memories of empathy and authentic purpose the same memories Vespera had invoked as a shield during the final confrontation.

Nightingale offered the crucial emotional stabilization. He sat by Minerva's side, reading her old journals and speaking of their laughter, their defiance, and the battles they had won together. His constant presence embodied loyalty and trust the human anchors Minerva needed to feel safe enough to return from the depths of her own mind.

After weeks of tireless, intensive effort, the Curative Pulse finally broke through Minerva's self-imposed barrier. She awoke her eyes clear but shadowed by the exhaustion of a soul that had wrestled with absolute control.

"The Monarch... he is Marcus Whitmore," Minerva whispered, her first words upon awakening. "The brother who sold his sister's soul for the promise of immortal control. He sees the chaos of love and grief as weakness to be erased."

Minerva's recovery transformed the Academy. She became living proof of the human mind's resilience and its first recovered patient. Her return allowed the Society to shift entirely into its educational and curative mission.

She soon developed the *Empathic Reintegration Protocol* a specialized psychic therapy designed to heal the thousands of victims left scarred by the D.O.R. and the Manufactured Memory program. Her method used controlled empathetic communication to help victims recognize and remove the artificial memories embedded in their minds, teaching them to trust the authenticity of their own thoughts once more.

With Minerva healed and Crowthorne stabilized (now residing at the Academy as a silent testament to their sacrifices), the Luminous Academy began its formal expansion. Their future no longer lay in secrecy, but in open education and transparent defense.

The Academy's headquarters a renovated Georgian townhouse became a beacon for those who understood the invisible war. Its faculty embodied experience and purpose:

- **Vespera Luminaire, Director of Synesthetic Defense:** She taught the visual detection of Silver Frequency contamination and trained students in counter-resonance shielding. Her Creative Sight became the foundation of all future protective technologies.

- **Aurelius Grimwald, Professor of Esoteric Countermeasures:** He formalized the occult arts of defense, teaching students to harness natural spiritual energies and ancient sigils to create psychic isolation wards and protective artifacts against technological mind control.

- **Detective Inspector Marcus Nightingale, Head of Forensic Psychology:** He established the methodology for identifying social and psychological vulnerabilities the Society had exploited turning detective work into an ethical science of resistance against manipulation.

- **Minerva Blackheart, Director of Empathic Reintegration:** She led advanced psychic defense, applying her Empathic Reintegration Protocol to heal victims of manufactured memories and train ethical psychic communicators.

The first students were drawn from Grimwald's wide network disillusioned academics, perceptive mediums, and engineers who had witnessed the strange electromagnetic events of the Night of Awakening. The curriculum emphasized ethical transparency, ensuring that the power of consciousness research would serve only defense and healing.

The Luminous Academy soon became the world's foremost defense against the Society of Perpetual Consciousness. The Monarch, Marcus Whitmore, had escaped to rebuild his empire but he faced a world now forewarned. Reports arrived from across the globe: similar organizations, inspired by his brief success, were rising. The fight against the Silver Frequency was far from over.

Vespera stood by the window of the Academy, her Creative Sight embracing London's endless, chaotic energy. She saw honest thoughts, bright hopes, and the complex struggles of millions. The Monarch saw chaos. Vespera saw unconquerable freedom.

The final battle had been won through the power of human ingenuity and chaotic love. The Luminous Society was ready. Their mission was eternal: to ensure that humanity's greatest asset, the infinite, free spirit of the individual mind would never again be claimed by those who sought to rule through control.

25

THE MONARCH'S RETURN

The Luminous Academy had become the nerve center for the final global campaign against the Silver Monarch. The war had evolved from physical confrontation to strategic defense aimed at rendering Marcus Whitmore's insidious vision of psychic control obsolete. Vespera, Grimwald, and Nightingale finalized their synchronized assault on the Monarch's new hub in Zurich while managing the escalating threat of rogue Manufactured Memory factions across Britain.

The Luminous Society's strategic division was essential. Grimwald, along with a cohort of the Academy's first students, the Consciousness Protectors departed for Edinburgh. Their mission was to dismantle a rogue operation attempting to resurrect the Manufactured Memory program using remnants of the technology stored in ancient vaults. Grimwald's team, equipped with advanced Counter-Resonance Shields and occult isolation techniques, focused on curative intervention ensuring the victims of memory corruption were healed, not harmed.

Detective Inspector Nightingale prepared for a high-stakes infiltration of the Monarch's financial hub in Zurich. Posing as an internal auditor investigating illegal transfers, he aimed to gain access to the Monarch's operational center hidden deep within a heavily shielded banking headquarters. His objective was not direct confrontation, but intelligence: locating the precise time and coordinates of the Monarch's next global launch window.

Vespera remained at the Luminous Academy in London, undertaking the most critical and complex task constructing the first full-scale Creative Pulse Shield. Using the Academy's advanced power grid and salvaged D.O.R. technology, she worked tirelessly to build a vast, protective electromagnetic barrier capable of neutralizing the Monarch's subtle, long-range suppression waves. Her Creative Sight became the ultimate tuning mechanism, aligning the Shield's chaotic frequency with the natural, unpredictable divergence of human thought.

The challenge was monumental. The Monarch's Silver Frequency was designed to be undetectable moving through the atmosphere like thought itself. Vespera's Shield had to be everywhere at once, a constant, silent defense field safeguarding the creative freedom of Britain's entire population.

Nightingale's infiltration of the Zurich banking fortress, a citadel of financial security wrapped in psychic shielding was both meticulous and perilous. He quickly uncovered the devastating scope of the Monarch's empire: millions of pounds were being funneled across the globe to fund decentralized Consciousness Nodes in major cities throughout Europe and Asia.

The Monarch's core objective became clear using the stability of the Swiss financial system as a platform for a global psychological war.

Deep beneath the headquarters, Nightingale found the Monarch's private operational chamber a soundproof, heavily shielded vault guarded by both armed security and a constant field of Silver Frequency suppression designed to neutralize unwanted consciousness or inquiry. Inside, Marcus Whitmore the Silver Monarch sat composedly at a massive command console. Though aged, he radiated a chilling, focused vitality. His eyes bore the cold detachment Vespera had once described from the New York vault. He was coordinating the global Society, wielding technology and capital with terrifying precision.

Whitmore smiled, instantly recognizing his visitor.

"Inspector. Your persistence is remarkable. Did you truly believe a police officer could dismantle the work of the global financial elite?"

"Your work ends here, Whitmore," Nightingale said, his pistol drawn.

Whitmore laughed a dry, mirthless sound. "End? No. It accelerates. The Consciousness Crown was a flawed prototype. My new devices are smaller, decentralized, and infinitely more elegant. They target individuals, not populations gradually eliminating creative divergence across key sectors: science, media, and finance."

He revealed his true goal not chaos, but absolute order. Whitmore intended to rebuild the world into a perfectly efficient market, governed by predictable, non-creative thought.

Nightingale realized he couldn't simply destroy the equipment. The decentralized network would instantly adapt. He needed the Monarch's launch window.

"The moral vacuum you operate in is staggering, Whitmore," he said, stalling for time. "You sacrificed your own sister, Margaret, for this warped ideology."

Whitmore's composure faltered.

"Margaret's mind was disorganized, inefficient! She chose chaos! We offered her perfect order, and she rejected it! I ensured her latent energy served a higher purpose the creation of a predictable future."

The distraction bought Nightingale the minute he needed. Locating the system's core timing array, he transmitted the data back to London through a disguised, high-frequency antenna hidden in his watch. The final coordinates for the Monarch's next global suppression wave were secured.

Back at the Luminous Academy, Vespera received Nightingale's transmission. The Monarch's launch window was four hours away.

Working beside the silent, catatonic Crowthorne whose blank mind served as a flawless model of uninfluenced consciousness Vespera initiated the final stage of the Creative Pulse Shield's deployment.

The Shield was designed to be non-lethal: a constant,

ambient field of pure creative chaos. It projected the electromagnetic signature of human unpredictability across the British Isles, jamming the Monarch's suppression waves before they could reach their targets.

Vespera closed her eyes, her Creative Sight spanning the vast, chaotic energy before her. She fine-tuned the final adjustments, channeling the creative chaos of London's free thought the jazz, the political dissent, the irrational love into the defensive field. The Shield rose, silently bathing the Isles in a subtle current of unconquerable ingenuity.

In Edinburgh, Grimwald and his team dismantled the rogue Manufactured Memory program, stabilizing its victims and retrieving key schematics to ensure the Monarch could not easily rebuild it.

Meanwhile, Nightingale escaped the Zurich vault, transmitting his data to authorities who swiftly froze the Monarch's assets, cutting off the financial lifeblood of the Society of Perpetual Consciousness.

The Silver Monarch was never captured, but his final global suppression wave failed. The Creative Pulse Shield held strong, preserving the creative freedom of the British Isles.

The Luminous Academy emerged as the world's first formal institution dedicated to Consciousness Protection. Though the Monarch financially crippled and technologically exposed retreated into the shadows, the Luminous Society remained vigilant.

Their mission was eternal: to safeguard the beautiful, chaotic, and utterly free spirit of the human mind.

EPILOGUE

THE ETERNAL DAWN

Six months after the final confrontation in Zurich, the Luminous Academy thrived within its shielded compound in Bloomsbury. The crisis of the Consciousness Crown and the collapse of the D.O.R. had sparked a global awakening forcing a quiet political reckoning with the realization that free will was a resource constantly under threat.

Vespera Luminaire, her Creative Sight now calm and sharply focused, oversaw the Academy's expansion. She worked tirelessly on the Creative Pulse Shield, refining its chaotic frequency to protect nations across Europe from the subtle suppression waves still emanating from rogue elements of the Society of Perpetual Consciousness.

Minerva Blackheart, now fully recovered, had become the Academy's spiritual pillar. She led the Empathic Reintegration Protocol, helping thousands of victims of the D.O.R. and the Manufactured Memory programs. Using her own traumatic experience as guidance, she helped others rediscover their authentic selves proving that even the deepest scars of the psychic war could be healed.

Aurelius Grimwald managed the Academy's security and global intelligence network, blending his ancient knowledge seamlessly with modern counter-electromagnetic technology. He trained a new generation of Consciousness Protectors, instilling in them the vigilance required to confront an enemy that believed in absolute technological order.

Detective Inspector Marcus Nightingale, now officially retired from Scotland Yard, served as the Academy's Chief Strategist. He maintained his global contacts, ensuring the political and legal defense of the Academy against the remaining power of the Monarch family, who used their dwindling wealth to destabilize global oversight.

The most haunting transformation was seen in Barnaby Crowthorne. He remained at the Academy, his body healthy, his mind silent. He had become its living monument: a reminder that genius without ethics leads only to annihilation. His quiet presence stood as a moral anchor, fueling the Academy's unwavering commitment to the ethical defense of human thought.

The work was relentless. Reports arrived daily bizarre psychological collapses in Hong Kong, strange behavioral shifts within a French political party, and the constant threat of the Silver Monarch's resurgence.

Marcus Whitmore the Monarch himself, though crippled financially and technologically exposed, had not been defeated. He remained free: a powerful, vengeful intelligence plotting his next move from the shadows. His influence was visible in the rise of imitation suppression technologies rogue scientists and financiers exploiting the D.O.R.'s abandoned blueprints.

The Luminous Academy now stood as the world's frontline defense.

Vespera's latest research centered on developing portable Creative Pulse Amulets small, wearable devices that generated localized fields of unpredictable thought, shielding their wearers from sudden psychic suppression.

Minerva's therapy sessions revealed a chilling truth: victims of Manufactured Memories remained deeply susceptible to renewed psychic attacks, requiring lifelong vigilance against the Monarch's lingering influence.

Grimwald's global network confirmed that the Monarch was now targeting the very systems of ethical oversight the Academy had fought to establish, using political manipulation and financial instability to erode their legal protections.

At last, a sobering understanding settled over the Luminous Society: their struggle was no longer against a single machine or man it was a perpetual, philosophical battle for the soul of humankind.

Vespera stood by the window of the Academy, her Creative Sight embracing the city's boundless energy. She saw the vast, chaotic, beautiful tapestry of human thought the very unpredictability the Monarch sought to erase.

She turned to her companions: Minerva, healed and resolute; Grimwald, wise and watchful; and Nightingale, steadfast as ever. In that moment, she knew their true victory was already won. They had chosen to protect the unpredictable, messy, and wonderfully human essence of free thought.

The war against the Society of Perpetual Consciousness would continue. The Monarch would rise again. But the Luminous Academy was ready.

They were the living, breathing defense against the tyranny of engineered thought a testament that the human spirit, in all its chaotic glory, remained the most powerful force in the universe.The Consciousness Protectors were prepared.

The future was unpredictable, free, and waiting.

ALSO BY CHARLES ETHERIDGE

The Luminous Society Series

- **Book 1:** *When The Radio Whispers*
- **Book 2:** *The Silver Frequency*
- **Book 3:** *The Memory Merchants*
- **Book 4:** *The Consciousness Crown*
- **Book 5:** *The Final Frequency*

Standalone Supernatural Thrillers

- *The Edinburgh Haunting*
- *Ghosts of the Industrial Revolution*
- *The Whitechapel Frequency*

THE SILVER FREQUENCY

A Luminous Society Novel – Book Two

The Luminous Society believed they had ended the threat of consciousness manipulation forever.

They were wrong.

When reports surface of an underground network helping consciousness manipulation victims escape Britain, Vespera Luminaire and her allies uncover a conspiracy that reaches far beyond government laboratories. Someone is using modified electromagnetic technology to build an army of "liberated" minds people who believe they've been freed, but are in fact programmed with entirely new identities.

As their investigation leads from the mansions of Edinburgh to the industrial heart of northern England, the Luminous Society discovers an international web of consciousness manipulators, each interpreting Crowthorne's research in their own dangerous way. The silver-topped walking stick has become a symbol of power in a shadow economy that trades in stolen thoughts and manufactured memories.

But the greatest threat may come from within. When Minerva Blackheart begins experiencing memories that aren't her own, the Society must face the terrifying possibility that their victory in London came at a cost they've only begun to understand.

Some frequencies, once heard, can never be silenced.

Some silver can never be tarnished.

And some minds, once touched by manipulation, may never be entirely their own again.

ABOUT THE AUTHOR

Charles **Etheridge** is a British author specializing in historical supernatural thrillers. Educated at Cambridge, where he studied both electrical engineering and historical occultism, **Etheridge** brings a unique, meticulous perspective to stories that blend scientific innovation with otherworldly phenomena.

His fascination with early broadcasting technology began during his graduate research into the pioneers of electromagnetic communication. This research sparked his enduring interest in the intersection between scientific discovery and spiritual belief that defined the early twentieth century.

Etheridge's work has been praised for its meticulous historical accuracy and atmospheric portrayal of 1920s

London. He is particularly noted for his authentic depiction of the era's technological advancements and the social tensions between traditional spiritualism and emerging scientific understanding. When not writing, **Etheridge** can be found maintaining an amateur radio station from his home in the Cotswolds.

ABOUT THE PUBLISHER

MK Storyworks is a truly global book publisher, dedicated to the timeless mission of connecting compelling authors with enthusiastic readers across the world.

We pride ourselves on curating a diverse and dynamic list that spans the full spectrum of literary interests. Whether you are looking for an immersive escape into a bestselling fiction novel, seeking wisdom and knowledge from groundbreaking non-fiction titles, perfecting a dish with our acclaimed cookbooks, or introducing the magic of reading to the next generation with our enchanting children's books, MK Storyworks delivers stories that inform, entertain, and inspire.

Our commitment to quality, creativity, and global reach ensures that every book we publish finds its place in the hands and hearts of readers, no matter where they are.

Connect with MK Storyworks

Stay up-to-date with our latest releases, author news, and behind-the-scenes glimpses by connecting with us online:

Website: www.mkstoryworks.com

Social Media:

- YouTube: @mkstoryworks
- Instagram: @mkstoryworks
- Facebook: @mkstoryworks
- X: @mkstoryworks
- Pinterest: @mkstoryworks
- TikTok: @mkstoryworks